The Aquar

by

Lisa Buck

Artwork by Zulf @Remmbrat

ISBN: 9798828088447

www.publishnation.co.uk

Prologue

Most moral virtues fall at the mean between two accompanying vices.
Let's use Pride as an example. Curb pride too much and you create the vice of deficiency. You are said to be timid. By not curbing it enough, you create the vice of excess. Then you are said to be conceited. The virtuous mean is Self Confidence. It's a very fine line.

Chapter 1
CHRIS

Pressing the fingertips of his index and middle finger to his lips before kissing them and turning his hand to make a peace sign towards the phone that he had just finished dialoguing to, Chris Lawrence hit the End Live button on the screen but not before giving his signature wink, huge white grin and mouthing "Peace" something he did at the end of every piece of content he created.

With the number of his followers in the hundreds of thousands across each of his social media platforms, daily vlogging was a huge part of Chris's personal brand. He had built an empire around this. No product. He was the asset. A personal brand with so many followers of his daily vlogs on You Tube, Instagram Stories, Tweets and Facebook lives, he was now the face of the agency he had created.

What started off as an idea mapped out on a pizza box in his bedroom when he was just 18, had taken twists and turns that he had never imagined and turned into the global phenomenon that it is today.

Sitting down behind a rack of stage lighting, a quick check on the reach statistics told him that his short live video posted yesterday promoting todays event had entertained an audience of 1.7 million people in less than 24 hours.

Feeling satisfied he looked up from his phone to find Jess, his P.A standing over him holding an i pad, wearing an earpiece and with a microphone sitting neatly on her cheek which was defined against her immaculately contoured make up.

Under one arm was tucked a very disgruntled looking Chinese Crested dog. His body completely devoid of hair apart from a wide tuft of white that spanned his bulging forehead and hung from his ears. It appeared to be wearing what looked like fluffy boots but were actually his four feet. Around his bald neck hung a patent black leather collar threaded with the silver letters F.I.D.E.L encrusted with glinting black Swarovski crystals.

“Are you ready?” Jess said. It clearly wasn’t a question as Jess spun on her heel and hitching Fidel back up under her arm, marched to the end of a corridor where 4 steps led up to an opening in the wall.

Bright stage lights shone through the gap where the curtain was open. Jess stopped and placed the little dog on the floor, pulled out a ball of cotton wool from the pocket of her skinny black jeans and poked a piece into each of its ears.

“There” she said, standing herself upright, “That should stop him pissing all over the stage. It’s the screaming that scares him. This way, he wont hear it!” Wiping her hands together and flashing a forced grin that belied the confidence in her accomplishment because everyone knew the dog would go on stage and be terrified to the point of soiling itself in-front of the enormous audience that had gathered in the arena to hear Chris Lawrence. CEO of MEAN Media give his TEDx Talk.

“Can’t we leave him backstage?” said Chris, sharing her underlying doubt of the success of the cotton wool.

“No!” She hissed, looking around to check no one could overhear their conversation, even wrapping her hand around the almost invisible microphone that adorned the contour of her perfectly sculptured cheek bone.

“ He is part of your BRAND” she hissed. “If he really starts to have a melt down, you can say he has a fashion shoot booked so has to leave early, then I can nip out and grab him. He can go in his cage until we are done here” She shot the terrified dog a disdainful look.

Jess glanced down at the ipad and let go of the microphone. Putting a perfectly manicured finger to her earpiece, she replied to the voice in her ear. “okay, yup”

With a jerk of the head and flick of her eyes she gave Chris the signal to pick up the dog and climb the four steps. “You’re on”

Chapter 2
REBECCA

Stepping through the entrance in to the empty round space that the inside of the newly renovated Windmill offered, Rebecca Lynch caught the heavy door with her heel and swung it closed behind her with just enough force for it to gently clunk shut.

Carrying the cat basket containing Scoundrel, her large ginger cat, she let out a small sigh of relief. A rocking chair and a stack of moving boxes were in the centre of the room. Through the windows she could see the expanse of marshland that surrounded the old mill.

She had purchased the mill at an auction with the money from the sale of her family home.

Breathing in the sea air, she took in the view. She could see all she needed from here to find the inspiration for her book. An uninterrupted view across the heathland to the sea to the east, the RSPB Nature reserves that stretched northward just inland. To the west lay the small coastal village of Walberswick and to the south, nestled just beyond the sand dunes with a garden that led directly to the beach was a small but beautiful cottage.

The perfect writers hideaway.

Rebecca held the cat basket in front of her doing her best to keep it level against what seemed the best effort of it's occupant to tip it up and make his escape. She carefully walked up the first section of the huge wooden spiral staircase that snaked up the centre of the building to the first floor, the beautifully crafted kitchen.

She placed the cat basket down, rummaged in her handbag and pulled out two silver bowls and a metallic pouch. She filled one bowl with cool water and set it down on the floor. Then tearing the pouch open, she emptied the contents into the other bowl. Crouching down to the basket, Rebecca gently undid the straps that secured the door.

"Out you come Scoundrel" she sang to the fluffy, rather annoyed looking tom cat "Come and eat some lunch then you can explore our new home"

With only a few boxes of personal possessions to unpack, Rebecca was in no rush. She sat cross legged on the floor and watched the cat suspiciously exit his temporary prison. Edging slowly out, she could see the internal struggle the cat was having. Torn as he was between shooting for cover, exploring his new surroundings or heading for the food that had wafted into his awareness before the sight of it had.

Rebecca smiled, she knew Scoundrel. His motto was food over fear. As she expected, the cat's belly had won over curiosity and he slunk over to the silver bowl and began to eat, his front legs slowly giving at the elbows bringing his fluffy ginger head nearer the bowl, his tail flicking in displeasure at having his routine interrupted.

"Good Boy" she gave him a stroke, unfolded her legs and stood up. She continued up the staircase to the next floor which was the living room.

Sunlight flooded the room from the huge windows. There was a small wood burning stove on the far wall , two comfortable sofas were separated by a low coffee table.

One further turn up the stairs led to the bedroom. The double 4 poster wooden bed had been built in that very room. Her new mattress had been delivered and lay unwrapped, ready to be made up in the new crisp white linen that Rebecca had bought and brought with her. Nothing of the old flat would be allowed space here. The memories were enough.

Chapter 3
SADIE & JOHN

Sadie was 54. She had never dyed her hair which was now varying shades of silver, dark grey and white. It was, as she referred to it "an unruly mop"

Sadie, was what you would describe, if you were familiar with the term, as a Hedge Witch. Her garden, surrounded her beautiful cottage that was nestled away up a long track, on the edge of a small coastal village in Suffolk. On first glance, you would think the planting was as wild as her hair, but on closer inspection (or explanation if you bothered to ask) you would realise that everything was grown as nature intended.

But there was more order to what was growing than your eyes would have you believe.

Because although there were flowers in the vegetable patch and tall weeds winding their way up trees, unless you recognised Belladonna with its ornate purple flowers that produced dark glistening berries or the purple spotted stem, fern-like leaves and delicate white flowers of Hemlock or any other number of what's known as the Baneful herbs (baneful meaning harmful and destructive) you would have no idea that any number of these innocuous looking plants, could kill you stone dead in less than 24 hours.

She picked some peas and shoots from a trellis and dropped them into the large front pocket of the apron tied around her slender waste. Then moving on to the tomatoes that cascaded down on thick vines, she gently gave a twist to the ones that looked ripest. All but one gave way easily. She smiled.

"Thank you for offering me only the juiciest" she appeared to be talking to the plant. She turned back towards the house, the sun shone on her back as she slowly made her way back to her kitchen.

Walking back along the winding path between the tall pink Foxgloves and the bright blue Larkspur, Sadie paused periodically to smell the flowers or snap off a piece of deadwood.

She picked a piece of sage and rubbed it between her index and middle finger and thumb. As she was bringing her hand up to take in the heady scent, she inexplicably dropped the leaf and instead of smelling the herb, she kissed the tips of her fingers, then turned her hand and raised the two fingers up to make a V sign. She heard herself utter the work "Peace"

She stood very still. Her head tilted slightly back and ever so gently nodding.

In the kitchen, sitting at the small pine table, drinking a mug of tea was Sadie's Husband of 30 years. John Malone. He was listening to Gardeners Question Time on Radio 4.

Entering the kitchen, Sadie, placed the haul of fresh fruit and vegetables on the draining board beside the sink.

"I hear that girl has moved into Marsh Mill" said John as Sadie returned from the garden

"Would make a beautiful home that" he continued as Sadie slowly took off her apron and sat down on the empty chair opposite John at the table.

"Shame if it only gets used for parties on a weekend" he grumbled.

"I need you to come and write for me John" she interrupted. "We need to do it now"

John put down his mug and looked at her questioningly.

In all the years he had been writing down the words Sadie spoke while she was in meditation, there had never been any urgency about it.

Sadie had always said that it would be obvious what to do with the pages upon pages of transcript they had accumulated over the years, when the time came.

And apparently, that time had come.

Chapter 4
CHRIS

"Without further ado, please welcome to the stage and show your love for the talented, gifted and incredibly successful Founder and CEO of globally acclaimed MEAN Media, Mr. Christopher Lawrence"

The stage lighting fired into life and the track now synonymous with Chris and MEAN Media, blasted out around the venue.

Chris felt that sinking feeling in his gut that had replaced the buzz of excitement he used to feel before stepping out on stage. He stooped down, picked up Fidel and muttered "Sorry boy" as he felt the little dog tense in his arms.

With a deep breath and a forced smile Chris strode, chest out onto the stage. 20,000 people packed into the O2 caught their first glimpse of the handsome, tall, muscular figure and his now infamous dog and erupted into cheers and screams that were bordering on hysteria.

Fidel immediately lost control of his bladder and pissed all down the side of the £1500 pound black tee shirt Chris had picked up in Gucci that morning.

The story Chris told onstage was titled "The Rise and Rise of my Authentic Self". He walked the audience through his story of how he started his business by meeting likeminded teenagers, who like him, had build huge followings across various social media platforms from the sanctity of their own bedrooms.

He had then encouraged them quit their mundane lives, pool their resources and join him on his journey. The crowd hung on his every word, barely taking their eyes off him to look at the accompanying screen presentation.

He told of how he often went hungry as he struggled to get his business off the ground until one day he managed to secure a huge Investment from Drew Dexter, a wealthy business man who was so impressed with how Chris pitched his idea so eloquently and with such passion, said he didn't care what the idea was.

With that all encompassing drive that Chris possessed, he wanted in.

With a ready built social media audience, whose combined following ran into the millions across the globe, MEAN Media was created.

Young geeky kids flocked from behind their lap tops to join the ever growing family that MEAN Media offered. They were given huge sums of money for control over the pages they had created and more importantly, their loyal following of millions of people.

The speed in which the success of MEAN Media grew was beyond anyone's wildest expectations. In the space of just 7 years, what started off as a scribble on a pizza box in the lodgings of his university accommodation had morphed into the fastest growing, most profitable and highly regarded agency in the world.

The big players were flocking to MEAN to run their social media campaigns. Exactly as Chris had planned.

His mission (he told the enraptured audience) was to show young people full of entrepreneurial spirit that it didn't matter where you came from, fortune favours the brave. Get up at 4am and hit the gym. Starve if you have to, but never give up. Work as hard as you can. Your success would be defined by your hustle.

That they too could easily obtain the Instagram lifestyle they longed for. The newest Range Rover, the Penthouse Apartment, the far flung destination vacations. Dare to be different until it payed off or die trying. Keep up the daily grind and they too could obtain the life he was living. The private jets, penthouse apartments and expensive sports cars.

What he failed to mention was, all of those things he thought would bring feelings of achievement had all turned out to be hollow and meaningless and he was so deep into his brand now he had no idea how to get out.

Chris kissed his fingertips and raised the peace sign to the crowd and made his way off stage. His talk had become so automated that he had spent the last few minutes not thinking about what he was saying as that was already so well versed. What Chris had been thinking, almost wishing, was to find a way to stop this feeling of dishonesty. He was losing control and didn't like that one little bit.

Chapter 5
REBECCA

Rebecca, just 12 when her Dad left, was often at home alone while her Mum worked. Having been left to bring Rebecca up on her own after her Husband left her for another woman 10 years her senior, Rebecca's Mother had worked hard to pay off the mortgage on the 2 bedroom terraced house on the edge of East London.

Fascinated by nature with a deep love of animals she would spend as much time outside as she could. It was just a 5 minute walk from her house to the edge of Epping forest. She would spend hours following the sandy bridleways that weaved their way through the trees, imagining what it would feel like to be one of those fortunate girls who rode past her on their ponies and wondering how it felt to gallop, laughing and shrieking across those long grassy plains that led to the little pub nestled on the edge of the woods.

Back at home, she escaped from her loneliness by writing stories. Creating new worlds full of characters she both loved and loathed in equal measure. Envious of their ability to become whatever they wanted with just a spark of inspiration and a few flicks of a pen from her. She longed to be able to create that ability for herself. That with something as simple as a thought, she could be living a life of her choosing with whatever opportunity she desired laid right out in front of her to take as and when she chose.

Her passion for writing never left her, so it was inevitable that she would become a writer of some sort when she grew up.

When Rebecca was 18, her Mum dropped a bombshell and told her she wanted to move away from London. Escape the old house and the painful memories it held. She needed peace and tranquility that wasn't to be found in London. She could rent the house out, continue to pay her mortgage and still have enough to live on. She was moving to Wales.

Rebecca understood why her Mum needed the space and time to sort herself out. In the six years since her divorce, she had worked constantly to keep the roof over their heads and cause as little disruption to her daughter as possible all the while doing her best to stave off the pain she felt about the break up of her marriage. Now Rebecca was finishing her A levels and would be seeking full time employment her Mother felt she could finally step back and take time for herself and deal with all the emotional baggage she had kept packed away so she could continue as normal a life as possible until Rebecca was old enough to stand on her own two feet.

Rebecca had barely seen her Father since he left, apart from when he would occasionally drop by to show off his new car, or photo's of the latest holiday he had been on with the new wife. One particular day he had appeared outside their house. Bibbing the horn on his latest purchase, a silly little convertible car that was more suited to a twenty something Hairdresser that an overweight man on the wrong side of 50. Rebecca saw him from the kitchen window, rolled her eyes and prepared herself for the barrage of bragging he had undoubtedly come round to inflict on her.

Walking out to the pavement, he signalled her to get in the passenger side. Obeying his request, Rebecca reluctantly got in.

Sure enough, without even bothering to wait for her to reply when he asked "You alright?" Before beginning to hand over photo's of his latest holiday, this time it had been a beach holiday in Tunisia.

He showed pictures of him and his new wife, riding skinny little Arab horses on a beach, tanned and laughing. Rebecca's stomach grumbled. Her Mum wasn't due to be paid until the end of the month. There was no food in the house and apart from half a jam sandwich she had made earlier that day after carefully removing a few spots spots of mould from the last slice of bread, Rebecca hadn't eaten all day.

The hunger pangs turned into anger and begun to rise from her stomach. How could he sit there, so proud of himself, showing photo's of beautifully presented plates of food when she and her Mother were barely scraping by.

"You could have a life like this Bec, if you play your card right" he preached.

Rebecca knew what was coming. She had heard it a million times.

" Find the right bloke to marry you and you'll be made" Rebecca gritted her teeth until her jaw began to ache. Growing up, the amount of things that Rebecca was told not to do or "No one will want to marry you" was a list as long as her arm. "Don't eat all that, you'll get fat. No one will want to marry you" or "Just do as you're told! No one will want to marry you if you argue back all the time" was another common one.

She wondered if her Dad was part of some secret society of men who were raising their Daughters to be obedient little wives. He would rather feed his super inflated ego by having a child he could brag to his friends about based on the car they drove, or the size of the house they owned rather than being proud of the independent strong women he had fathered.

"Keep yourself looking nice, don't let yourself go, find yourself a rich man and do everything you can to hang on to him" was today's nugget of advice.

He never once told her that he loved her. Never once did he make her feel valued as the person she was, only ever telling her what not to do. Like get fat or go out looking like a frump. Rebecca had heard enough. She was hungry. She was obviously not good enough for him to want to hang around with apart from when he wanted a captive audience to brag to.

She opened the car door "Bye Dad" She said feeling utterly deflated. Climbing out of the car and standing herself up straight, at only 5ft 5 she still seemed to tower over the tiny sports car where her Father sat, his hair dyed, sunglasses on, belly spilling onto his lap.

That had been the last contact she had with him.

Weighing up the opportunities Wales had to offer in contrast to staying in the capital was a no brainier. The only part that made it hard was having to be separated from her cat, Scoundrel. Obviously he couldn't move with her so it was agreed that the fluffy ginger menace as he was affectionately known, would move with Rebecca's Mum and take up the role terrorising the Welsh wildlife of his new surroundings.

Rebecca applied for a vacancy as a Telephonist in a central London hotel.

She managed to blag the job by saying in her interview she had experience in operating a telephone system, only to have to dig herself out of her lie when faced with the switchboard. The job came with accommodation. A room in the staff hostel, which was a 6 storey house located just around the corner from the hotel.

Taking up every opportunity for overtime offered in other departments, waiting tables and working occasional bar shifts, she was able to earn enough money to pay for an open university course in Freelance Journalism.

Over the next 3 years, Rebecca had numerous articles published on places to go in London, sharing discount codes given to her by the club owners to entice guests from the hotel to spend their money in their gaudy establishments.

She was getting her name known but missed the satisfaction she got from creatively writing. On a whim, she sent an example of her Girl About Town diary to the Editor of a London paper, in which she had created her character, Suzie. A sleek, 20 something rich girl, who lurched through the week practicing Yoga by day and struggling to remaining upright by night. Swinging from one Night-club to the next, consuming vast amounts of vodka and smoking copious amounts of cigarettes. Rebecca had started writing Suzie diaries when she first moved to London. Between shifts at the hotel and writing her Where to Go reviews, Suzie had been her only creative outlet.

The Editor loved what she read and called Rebecca the very next day to offer her a weekly column. Suzie. Girl

About Town was a popular read. Her diaries were bursting with tales of expensive shopping trips, boozy lunches, embarrassing drunken mishaps and disastrous dates. With the extra income, Rebecca was able to leave the staff accommodation and move into a flat share on the Edgeware Road. Sharing a kitchen, living room and bathroom with a guy called Patrick, a 6ft 6 black guy, also from London who, when he wasn't waiting tables at a coffee shop on Bond Street, morphed in Angie Feather, Drag Queen Extraordinaire who had a huge fan base at his regular haunt, Madame Jo Jo's.

And then there was Gus. He was funny and sweet. He had a sadness about him that stemmed from an illness that has caused him to leave the job he loved .He had been a Police Officer for just 3 years when he caught meningitis. The virus that left him with a form of epilepsy. It wasn't severe but serious enough to mean he couldn't carry out the job in the direction he wanted his career to go in, so was forced to leave.

He found a job as Head of Hotel Security and had felt stuck there ever since.

Over the next 5 months Rebecca and Gus spent most of their free time during the week together when his shifts allowed. She would cook for him and started to look after him, making sure he had clean shirts, that his work suits were collected from the cleaners and eventually, sharing her bed with him. She allowed herself to daydream about Patrick moving out and the large flat becoming just theirs. At the weekend, Gus would visit his parents in Hertfordshire leaving Rebecca to fill her time alone.

Occasionally she would visit her Mum in Wales where she had met and settled down with Robert, a landscape gardener. She, along with Scoundrel had moved into Robert's cottage and were living their best lives. Her pottering around the small garden and making jam from fruit she had grown and Scoundrel keeping the local mouse population to a minimum.

But more often than not, Rebecca would stay in London and walk to Kensington Gardens to sit under a shelter, retreat into her mind and create more characters for the pages of the novel she still hadn't gotten around to writing.

It was around 7pm on a cold, rainy Friday night in February. Rebecca with hands and arms full of shopping bags from Sainsbury's, struggled to open the front door to the flat. She could hear the house phone ringing. Finally managing to locate her keys in her bag and then retrieving them from the lock, she stepped though into the long hallway, dropping the bags and dripping rain all over the tiled floor, turning to push the door shut with her foot.

The flat was in darkness. Patrick had obviously not yet made it home from the coffee shop. Gus had told her that morning that he was packing his weekend bag to take to work so he could leave straight from his shift to catch the train to his parents for the weekend.

A smile crept over her face as she remembered that morning. How Gus had looked her straight in the eye, his hand on her cheek as he told her " you are so special to me you know" . Rebecca's heart had skipped a beat and she wanted the moment to last forever but had instead playfully whacked him with the pillow from her bed and made a swift exit for the shower, calling him a soppy twat. Embarrassed at his show of emotion and torn between wanting to hear more and the discomfort of someone showing her affection.

The phone stopped ringing.

Shaking off her coat and kicking off her soaked boots, she picked up the shopping and padded down the hall to the kitchen. She flicked on the light and heaved the bags up onto the worktop. An envelope was propped up against the toaster. Just her name was handwritten on the front. Frowning she picked it up and tore open the sealed flap.

She read.......

Rebecca,
I am so sorry to do this to you. I cant do this anymore. This isn't an easy decision. I am leaving. I have packed my stuff and am moving back home.

I never meant to fall in love with you. I should have never let it happen. Things just got out of control and you are so so lovely and you have been looking after me so well. But I can't carry on because its just not fair on either of us.

The truth is Bec (she hated her name being shortened but had let him get away with it because she thought it was something special between just them) the truth is, I have a girlfriend. And I never meant for things between us to get this far but me and her, well we are getting married....

The phone began to ring again, but she didn't hear it at first.

Her head was filled with a rushing sound, like when you are on a fast train and it enters a tunnel. But the fast train of thoughts in her head exited the tunnel and the ringing of the phone began to filter through.

There were more words on the page, but as the ringing registered followed by the realisation it could be Gus calling her to tell her he had made a mistake, not to read the letter, she turned and ran, sliding on the wooden floor in her socks to make it to the phone in the living room. She grabbed up the receiver

"Gus?"

"Rebecca?, Is that you?" The deep welsh male voice on the other end of the phone asked.

"Robert?, yes its me but this isn't a good ti"....she paused.

Why was Robert calling "Is everything ok Robert, where's Mum?"

She heard him stifle a sob " Rebecca, darling. I'm so sorry. It's your Mum. I came home from work and found her. She was in the garden darling. They think it was an aneurism in her brain"

The room spun and Rebecca fell against the wall. "Is she, is she okay?"

Another stifled sob down the line "Darling, I'm so sorry. She was already dead when I found her. She's gone my love. I'm so sorry. Your Mum has gone"

Her Mums funeral had been the hardest day of her life so far. Held in the little village where her Mum had made her new life, she sat at the front of the church, accompanied by Patrick and his on off partner Vincent.

She looked and felt so much smaller than she actually was. Not only because she was flanked by them who were both close to 7ft. The sobbing figure of Robert to her left, who's large strong frame was wracked with stifled sobs.

Throughout the short service she kept her eyes averted from the coffin and not until the burial was almost over did she force herself to look at the wicker casket that held her Mum's body as she stepped forward to throw the first handful of dirt onto it.

The months that followed were almost unbearable for Rebecca to endure. Supported by Patrick and his wonderful eclectic group of friends who made sure she ate something every day, called round on the pretence of visiting Patrick when they knew full well he was at work but invited themselves in anyway and then proceed to tear Gus a new arsehole, ranting at his disgraceful behaviour.

Although he had paid the landlord his share of the rent that was owed for his notice period, he had not made any contact with either Rebecca or Patrick. No one had any forwarding address for him either and obviously all attempts to contact him by phone had failed.

Rebecca had told Gus it was refreshing to meet someone who didn't use Social Media. Now it was obvious why he didn't. He had completely disappeared but Rebecca had no desire to track him down. To her he had become like one of those drinks you had once had such a good time drinking but then had made you so sick, just the mention of its name caused a gag reflex.

She continued to live in the flat while the sale of her childhood home went through. The Suzie diaries were falling out of favour as the chiefs were under pressure to keep clean living at the forefront of their articles, promoting a healthy lifestyle. More people were turning to plant based diets and Vegan living was becoming more of a thing to aspire to.

Everyone knew that the people reading the column identified far more with piss head Suzie who got wasted every weekend and ended up throwing up in her handbag in the back of an Uber but not before deftly pulling out the last wrap of cocaine from the lining so as not to ruin it.

With Suzie looking like she needed a break from being Girl About Town and more Girl In Rehab, Rebecca made the decision to do exactly that.

She spoke to her editor who agreed that putting fictional Suzie into a stint of fictional rehab would leave the door open for her to return in the future. Maybe coming back as a vegan Life Coach. Much more in keeping with the Instagram life the paper's readers pretended to live. So Suzie was promptly ensconced in The Priory to sort her shit out.

With the house sale completed (which went for an exorbitant amount) Rebecca was able to buy an old converted windmill by the sea where she could live off the remainder of the money and finally allow herself the breathing space to write her book.

Chapter 6
SADIE & JOHN

Sadie had been 24 when she and John met. She was working in the local pub in the little village of Walberswick, where Sadie grew up. John had been visiting the area with a group of friends for the weekend.

The Anchor pub, where Sadie worked, had been recommended to John and his friends who had decided to stop there on their last day for lunch before heading back to London. He had been waiting at the bar to be served when his breath was taken away at the appearance of a strikingly beautiful, tall slender girl. Her hair was twisted into dreadlocks, there wasn't a colour on the spectrum that didn't appear somewhere in what she was wearing and she jingled as she moved due to the large number of silver bangles she wore.

Her nails were painted a silvery blue. The sunlight that shone through the front window of the pub was reflected by the large silver rings that were hanging in her ears. As if all that wasn't enough to take in, when she looked up properly, her eyes were mesmerising. The brightest green he had ever seen. He fell in love with her there and then.

Sadie, used to the gormless look that appeared across the faces of those who had not seen her before, stood opposite him on the business side of the old oak bar and waited for him to say something.

When no words came out of his slightly open mouth, she thought he needed snapping out of his shock. She was used to being stared at, even ridiculed for her weird hippy clothes and unusual hair. Her tastes in practically everything were so eclectic that there was no label that could be attached to her style. She was just Sadie Myers. Barmaid. Lover of animals, vegan, earth warrior and living a peaceful, carefree life.

She lived alone in her rented cottage on the edge of the village. She grew most of her own food and the money she made from working in the pub and occasionally selling her artwork provided all she needed to cover her rent and feed the array of animals that she took care of. She had everything she wanted right there in the village. Where most young people developed a wanderlust and a desire to see the world, Sadie was content to stay in the village she was born in and take care of the multitude of animals that almost constantly flowed her way.

Any wildlife that was found injured, limping or in a generally sorry state, would inevitably end up with Sadie until well enough to be released or in some cases, take up residence with her and live out their days in as natural an environment she could create for them. She did rely on certain neighbours for emergency lifts to the Vet in nearby Southwold as she didn't drive, she had never wanted to. Mostly, she was able to nurse whatever waif and stray came her way using natural remedies that she made from what she grew in her garden.

It was not unusual to see Sadie walking or cycling through the village with various animals following her or birds circling above her, following in her direction as she went to the beach or to the local post office. Everyone knew her locally and her calm, kind manner soon put to rest any preconceived ideas formed by first visual impressions.

She had been taught by her own Mother and Grandmother the ways of the Hedge Witch. Her aim in life was to, as she was taught, live as lightly on the earth as she could in the time she had here. Use what Mother Nature provided to live a clean and compassionate life. Born under the sign of Aquarius, the water carrier, Sadie was the epitome of an Aquarian. Often mistaken as a Water sign, Aquarians are air signs. The water represents emotions, both theirs and the emotions of others that they carry without it having an effect on them.

Sadie was an empath. She could immediately sense when something or someone was out of balance. It was like having a personal radar. She would feel the blip in her inner core before any words were spoken. Sadie felt imbalances often before the other person realised they were off kilter.

She would batch cook delicious, hearty soups and stews and put them in jars, and deliver them on her bike to various occupants within the village. Never accepting money but happy to trade for fruits or vegetables that she maybe wasn't growing at home. She also accepted food that the animals could eat. People often would leave bags of bird seed or a sack of mixed corn for the geese, ducks and ex battery hens that had taken sanctuary at Blyth Cottage with Sadie.

The besotted John, having been staring at Sadie for what felt like an eternity but was in fact less than 10 seconds, stuttered back into life, completely flustered and asked for 4 pints of Adnams.

"Right you are" said Sadie, relieved he had finally spoken. She was used to being stared at, but he wasn't even trying to hide it.

"Are you staying for Lunch?" She asked, "Only, I can bring your drinks over to your table if you want to run a bar tab"

"I'd love to stay for lunch" said John. Then he added "Everyday" without realising, he had said it aloud and not just in his head. Sadie burst out laughing.

Immediately, he flushed red and stepped back from the bar.

Did he really just say that? John, you fucking idiot, he scolded himself in his head. Wishing the floor would open up and swallow him. To save him from his embarrassment he did the next best thing and mumbled "er, yes, please, that would be great" while fumbling in his back pocket for his wallet "er....here" he handed over his card.

Sadie, reached out to take it and their fingers touched. They jumped in unison as they felt a bolt of energy shoot through both their hands. The card fell onto the bar. For a few seconds they looked into each others eyes, mirroring each other's expression, neither knowing what was happening but both feeling the intense atmosphere that was building.

Sadie broke her gaze first, and the silence. "I'll bring them over and I'll grab you some menu's. I've got to nip and change the barrel so I'll be a couple of minutes. I wont be long" and with that she jingled her way towards the cellar door.

John had turned and almost ran back to his table to rejoin his friends. Hoping they hadn't noticed what a complete tit he had just made of himself. But of course they had noticed.

"Oi Oi Johnny Boy" the 3 other men jeered as he neared the table.

"Fuck off" said John under his breath, still completely flustered. As he sat down he stole another glance back towards the bar. He felt numb. He had never met or seen a girl that had that effect on him. It was like a spell had been cast on him. He was utterly smitten.

Sadie, now down in the cellar, paused between changing the barrel over and became very still. A feeling hit her hard in her chest. A memory chimed in the back of her mind, but not anything clear enough to recollect. A bit like when you try and recall a dream and its in your memory somewhere, but you cant quite reach it. Could he be the one she had asked for? The one she had written about in her journal. The soul mate she was expecting? She shivered and pulled her multi coloured cardigan tight around her tall slim frame and turned her attention back to the job at hand.

So undeniably attracted to each other, for the next 4 weekends, John made the drive up from London where he lived and worked as a Carpenter, to spend as much time as he could with Sadie. They walked over the sand dunes that separated the village from the beach. Crossing the wooden bridge that spanned the estuary where the Blyth met the sea at Southwold Harbour and taking long walks along the beach holding hands and talking.

When they wasn't talking, the silences were far from uncomfortable. It was as if they continued communicating. Such was their connection that it didn't seem hasty or misguided for John to want to quit his job and move to Walberswick to be with Sadie every day. He could find work easily. A wood worker with his skills could work anywhere and of all the places in the world that he could think of, that little village on the coast was the only place he wanted to be. With the only person he was interested in spending any time with. His Sadie.

They married 6 months later.

Sadie brought out the spiritual side of John that he never knew existed. From watching her, how she lived with so much compassion and her unwavering belief in natural balance.

He began to question everything he had, up until then, taken as gospel. When he moved into Blyth Cottage with her, he felt the full force of her beliefs.

He began by laughing when she spoke to her plants. She wasn't having conversations with them, but always thanked them for what they provided, in return for her tending to them so beautifully. But when he really thought about it, why wouldn't you show appreciation? After all, if you don't feel gratitude when something you desire appears in your reality, doesn't that make you ungrateful?

Sadie talked endlessly about Universal Laws. The laws of rhythm and polarity and the one she philosophised about the most, The Law of Attraction.

The conversations they had in the evenings, sitting in front of the open fire were like nothing John had ever experienced. There are some who will never know the satisfaction and joy that comes from deep conversation. Real thought provoking ideas and philosophies.

Sadie was one of those people who felt before she thought. It's a step beyond think before you speak. Her Mum and her Gran had taught her this. They didn't believe in organised religion but practiced a way of life that had almost been forgotten. They practiced their connection to source energy.

It was only a few weeks after they met that John began to learn of this. Sadie, never guarded in her conversation because she had no shame or guilt in her belief, began to explain about Source Energy and how we are all connected. How we are all one shared consciousness. She talked about the vibrational energy of emotion and the power of your words and how you speak to yourself.

As much as he wanted to comprehend what she was saying, it didn't all make immediate sense. It was all new to him. His life had revolved around drinking in rough pubs. His idea of spirit was the kind that came out of the optics behind the bar. But over time and many intense discussions, having heard many explanations and seen many examples, it began to make sense to him.

Sadie never forced her beliefs on anyone. She knew that in order for something to feel pure in the mind, it had to come from having the freedom of choice. That is Human nature. Every action must be chosen freely and originate from within oneself. It cannot be imposed by others. All she did was shine a light in the direction of her beliefs, she never told John what to see. What he chose to believe must come from his freedom of thought and his own perception.

Sadie had rituals she performed. They were those, which throughout history had been vilified by those in pursuit of power. Because with power came control. And when Humans allow themselves to be controlled, they lose their freedom. That leads them to become disconnected from their inner being, their individual piece of source energy that dwells within them. And when that happens, their balance is disrupted. And without balance there is chaos.

Sadie loved to meditate. It was her sustenance. John's introduction to meditation was a pivotal point in his life. Feeling that life couldn't get any better, he gave no real credence to the possibility of further expansion but when he began to meditate he soon learned that his mind opened to possibilities almost beyond his comprehension.

His whole life changed. An entirely new way of life was shown to him and he embraced it fully.

He developed a calmness like which he had never known. He had always viewed calmness as a kind of weakness but Sadie was an example of how living a simple compassionate life brought more joy than any material thing or a personality filled with anger or frustration could provide.

The connection between them seemed it was forged long before the day they had met in The Anchor.

Within the first year of them being together, John had been offered more work than he could take on. His expertise and natural talent for both joining and carving wood, meant he had offers of work converting barns and working on listed timber frame buildings.

When the opportunity to purchase Blyth Cottage arose, they were able to buy it. From the sale of his small flat in London, he had more than enough equity in it to put down a decent deposit and manage a mortgage on the cottage.

John continued working which allowed Sadie the option to be less reliant on her wage from the pub. She spent more time looking after the garden which led to higher yields of fruit and vegetables. She would cook and make jams and chutneys that she sold from a little table at the end of the lane. A small tin honesty box was put out alongside the jars where people would post their payment for what they took.

She also had more time to paint and to meditate.

It was then that her stilled mind was able to cease all momentum of the mundane thoughts that generally occupied the mind of most people day to day. She opened her mind to a stream of ideas and inspirational thought. Almost like she was receiving them from an outside transmitter.

Without realising, Sadie had opened the door to channelling.

Chapter 7
CHRIS

Chris couldn't wait to change out of his dog piss soaked clothes. He stank. Holding his breath as he stepped into the lift of his apartment building on the South Bank of the Thames, he tapped his key on the control pad.

He felt beads of sweat forming along his hairline but he remained motionless, his hand on the rail, steadying himself as the elevator shot skywards.

He counted backwards. A trick he had learned to counterbalance the fear he felt as he was carried higher up the tall glass building. It only took counting rhythmically from ten down to one to reach his destination.

The doors had not finished opening before Chris had his leg through the door, stepping into the entrance hall of his penthouse apartment.

Performing his usual ritual, following the line of the marble floor tiles with his eyes to navigate his way to the centre of his open plan kitchen, all the while keeping his head down so as to avoid the panoramic view of the London Skyline.

Reaching the island in the centre of the room, Chris leant against it and inhaled deeply. He swung his laptop bag onto the counter and lay his phone down on its charging pad. His battery was running dangerously low.

Walking sideways from the kitchen, keeping his back to the window, he made it to the bedroom and the en-suite. He pulled off his tee shirt and pulled down his jeans to his knees, lifting his legs in turn to extract himself from the stinking damp denim. "Shower on" he said as he freed his last foot. The shower cascaded into life and within seconds steam was bellowing from behind the glass screen. Chris stepped into the shower and stood motionless as the intensely hot water ran in rivulets down his body.

He emerged 15 minutes later wrapped in a towel. He felt bad that he had left the O2 without giving time to his fans. He always made a point of staying behind after his speaking engagements, where queues of young people clamoured to take a selfie with him or beg him for the one piece of advice he could give that would set them on their own course for success.

The most commonly used piece of advice was to always be your authentic self.

Recently, Chris had found he had started coughing when he went to use that line. Almost like his throat was closing. He had been trotting out that saying for years, but just lately had he began cough. It was almost like he was subconsciously stopping himself from saying it aloud.

Fidel was scratching at the balcony door to be let out. Turning his back to the large glass doors that opened out onto the most sought after view in London, Chris shuffled his way backwards across the room, picking up his now fully charged phone. Arriving at the doors, arse first, he reached behind and unlocked then slid the floor to ceiling glass open.

A rush of cool air hit his back. Fidel hopped the threshold, took no more than 4 steps out onto the tiled floor of the enormous wraparound balcony and proceeded to squat.

Just beyond where Fidel was relieving himself, strings of bulbs illuminated a huge hot tub. The steaming bubbling water sounded so inviting. Chris knew that going live on Instagram from the tub always increased his viewing figures. #TubTime #AskMeAnything had become a weekly ritual. Closing his eyes and with a sigh of resignation Chris dropped to his hands and knees, and proceeded to crawl backwards across the tiles.

The balcony itself wrapped around the entire top floor of the exclusive building, encompassing the penthouse and accessible from almost every room. There were no railings to the edge of the expansive balcony, instead, to maximise the view that commanded the multimillion price tag, thick glass had been installed. It looked, even from close up like you could walk clean off the edge.

Being careful to avoid placing either his knees or hands on anything Fidel had deposited Chris worked his way backwards, following the lines on the tiles, like a memory map of a maze. Reaching the outer steps of the tub, still with his back to the invisible glass barrier, he pushed himself up into a squatting position and placed his backside on the lowest step of the tub. Keeping his eyes focussed on ground, he bumped his way up the steps until, now almost upright, he was sitting on the edge of the tub.

Taking a few slow breaths to steady himself, he twisted his body and swung his legs over and into the water. Closing his eyes, he straightened his body and still clinging to the edges, lowered himself down into the bubbling spa, being careful to hold his phone clear of the water while scooting to the far side of the tub and taking his place with his back to the open view which spread out behind him. Once he had steadied his breathing, he raised the phone and flicked on the reverse camera. Checking his hair was just enough hot tub ruffled, and his nose was clean of snot from sobbing in the shower less than half an hour earlier, Chris hit the Start Live Video button.

630,000 people watched in envy as the self made multi millionaire live streamed from the hot tub of his dream penthouse apartment while he exhorted his followers to strive harder to focus on working harder to achieve their goals.

It wasn't until he went to sign off with his signature finger kiss and peace sign, that he realised he had dog shit on his hand.

When Chris arrived in the office the next day there was more of a buzz around than usual. One of the campaigns was trending and was apparently "breaking the internet"

Looking down at the performance stats that Jess had handed him, he scanned down the page looking at the reach and comparing the performance of each post.

It was from a video campaign where Chris's face had been close up. His words punched up on the screen as he spoke. It was encouraging his followers to break away from the crowd. Hustle harder. Work later. Start earlier. Break the cast that had them set in their lazy ways. Succeed how he had.

Chris felt sick. He knew he couldn't continue like this. He was leading good, honest people into a life without meaning. Yes they might achieve monetary success.

Maybe. But he wasn't being honest and that felt wrong. Wrong to the point that he felt he had to get out right away. He needed to find a way out of this mess his personal brand had created.

Chris, made a clic clic sound in the direction of Fidel, who sprung to his feet. "C'mon boy, let's go" Grabbing his keys and and laptop and checking his pocket for his phone, Chris made his way through the huge glass doors of Mean Media and down the steps to the underground car park. On his way, he messaged Jess to say he had been called away on an emergency and wouldn't be back until Monday.

He stopped at his apartment building to retrieve some clothes and one small item he kept hidden in the bottom of his wardrobe in the penthouse, Chris slowly made his way through the traffic of Central London then East London where it met the M25. Fidel was curled up and gently snoring on the passenger seat. Chris with his mind whirling, began his journey towards Suffolk and the sanctity of his cottage by the sea.

Many things had been bothering Chris lately. Beyond the day to day hurdles of running a multi million pound global agency, things that ran deeper were beginning to surface. The feelings he suppressed by surrounding himself with the best that money could buy were no longer pacified by his material wealth. It was like squeezing a blade of a sharp knife in the palm of his hand while trying to distract himself from the pain with shiny objects, which had worked for a while but lately he was forced to bring his methods into question. He was being forced to call it all into question.

He arrived in the little coastal town of Walberswick in what seemed like record time as he rolled up on the entrance of the driveway. Now dusk, the headlights that had automatically switched on, picked up the front windows of the little cottage. Chris felt a wave of relief as he took the longest, calmest breath he had taken in a long while.

Scooping up Fidel and grabbing his laptop, Chris slammed and locked the doors of his shiny black Range Rover. Fumbling under a stone that lay beside the door mat, he located the key that his housekeeper had left out for him on request when he called her from the car as he left london and let himself in.

Taking in the familiar smell of his teenage years, he felt instant reassurance that he would find the answers. All he needed to do was quieten his mind, and this was exactly the right place to do that. He knew that without question. It was the only place he could really be himself.

After a fitful night's sleep, Chris woke up early. Rolling out of bed and opening the curtains, blinking at the sunrise that was climbing in the sky from beyond the horizon.

Squinting at the sun, looking out to sea from the upper window of his bedroom in the cottage, Chris decided he would take Fidel down to the beach before heading up to the shop to grab some supplies.

He opened the wardrobe and was faced with neat rows of clean, pressed tee shirts, piles of jeans and a stack of shorts. It felt warm so he went for the shorts, grabbed a tee shirt from a hanger and made his way downstairs.

By the door hung a small plain collar and lead. He picked it up and put it on Fidel, replacing the ridiculous black bejewelled one.

Shoving his bare feet into his trainers that he had left neatly by the door the night before Chris walked back through the house to the small kitchen, unlocked the backdoor and stepped out into the garden that lead right out onto the dunes.

Fidel stopped to piss up a pile of stones that lay at the boundary of the garden where it met the sand.

Chris strode up the dune and over the top where he got is first sight of the beach. It wasn't all soft sand, there was a big bank of stones that sloped down the towards the sea before giving way to soft sand and the water's edge. The waves lapped at the shore. Fidel had caught Chris up and was now yapping and chasing the seagulls that landed and just as he reached them, took off and swooped over his head, mocking the bald little dog, who was running free, without his famous collar.

Walking down to the edge of the sea, Chris took off his trainers and stepped into the water. The temperature took his breath away, even though just covering his ankles it was enough to send the chill up his legs and surge around his body.

He made a sharp intake of breath. Fidel was jumping up waiting for Chris to throw a stone for him to chase. Chris knew if Fidel went in the water he would get so cold he would have to carry him home and warm him back up. With no hair for protection, Fidel had to be protected from the cold. And from the sun. In fact, poor Fidel had to be protected from everything. It was a job Chris took on without complaint.

Since the night he had first seen him, a tiny puppy, being offered for sale by a junkie on the street, Chris had relished in the responsibility of taking care of Fidel. Chris, had pulled a fifty pound note from his pocket and handed it over. He couldn't leave that poor terrified defenceless puppy in the arms of his drug fuelled owner. The feeling he got from knowing he had saved him and been able to offer the little dog the most lavish lifestyle money could buy was worth much more to him than fifty pounds. However, it was obvious that Fidel wasn't happy with the situation that all that wealth brought. The media attention, hardly ever sleeping in the same city on more than two consecutive nights was the same feeling Chris himself had been struggling with.

The journey to get to where he was had been exciting and exhilarating but once he was there the feeling of achievement seemed short lived and nowhere near as pleasurable as the journey to create it. It hadn't brought the fulfilment he expected. No sooner had he hit one benchmark he was striving headlong towards the next. It wasn't that he didn't appreciate reaching his goals, but when he did, they became devoid of all meaning. They were hollow. Like him.

He had become increasingly aware that the life he was peddling and encouraging others to achieve wasn't the path to happiness he had fooled himself it would be. He had always thought the "Money cant buy happiness" saying was a pile of shit, made up to stop others wanting to share the wealth of the few. Although now it had begun to make sense. He hadn't allowed himself to contemplate that further because he knew deep down what it would mean.

Backing out from the shore's edge Chris and Fidel walked north along the beach, parallel to the marshes. Chris was not allowing himself to think about how he was going to address the issue Instead, he had decided he would enjoy this walk, fill himself with the peace of mind being here brought him then grab some breakfast on the way back and then set his mind to solving the problem.

Scanning the sand as he walked, Chris stopped and bent to pick up stones, looking for imprints of fossils. He didn't notice that Fidel had made his way up the stoney bank and beyond the wire fence line that separated the marsh from the beach.

When he stood up, having been crouching to examine a small piece of orange looking stone that he thought may be a piece of Amber, Chris looked around for Fidel. He couldn't see him. There was no where he could be hiding and Chris's gut lurched. He took off at a sprint up the stoney bank to gain a higher vantage point, calling Fidel at the top of his voice. From the top of the stones Chris caught sight of a fluffy white tuft of hair that was Fidel's tail, bolting across the Marshes in hot pursuit of what looked like a big ginger cat. Chris took off after him, the lead he had clipped to his shorts whacking his thigh as he ran. The fugitive dog appeared to be heading towards a Windmill on the marshes and Chris hoped that someone would catch him before he made it onto the road that led to the village beyond.

Chris, heart pumping was sprinting fast across the marshes. Ahead of him was Fidel, still chasing the cat. Their pathway highlighted by birds taking off in fear as the age old canine versus feline scenario played out in the direction of the tall white Windmill. Such was the panic that filled his chest that he was about to lose his little dog, who Chris realised, in truth was the only thing he really cared about in life.

Chris saw Fidel disappear around the side of the Windmill that was on the other side of the fence line.

Jumping the wire without breaking stride Chris's cries of "Fidel, Fidel stop" became more desperate as he lost sight of the little bald dog. When he reached the windmill and ran around the edge of it following the path the cat followed by the dog had taken he pulled up. He couldn't see him.

"FIDEL!" Shouted Chris. He tried to listen, desperate not to think about hearing a car screech but even if it had, he wouldn't have heard it over the sound of the blood pumping around his body. His own heartbeat filling his ears.

Not knowing which way to run next Chris pulled out his phone, pressed his thumb to the button and said breathlessly but as clearly as he could

" FIND MY DOG"

The phone responded in a clipped female English accent. "Would you like to track by map from your current location?

"YES" replied Chris

Squinting at the screen Chris watched the screen as a map popped up. He could see a blue drop pin that was marked You Are Here. About 1 mile back in the direction in which they had come at the edge of the beach where they had begun their walk was the flashing red beacon. Your Dog Is Here. Thats impossible murmured Chris, thats my cottage. He cant have made it ba..

and then it registered. He had swapped Fidel's collar that held the tracking device .

When he was just 10 years old Chris had been taken into care. His Mother was a wreck and he had never known his Father. He had been told that his real Dad had died after becoming involved in a fight in a multi story car park that had resulted in him falling from the top level of the building. His injuries so severe that he wasn't able to be identified by his next of kin. Of course this information he had learned at school. Gossip in the playground was all he had to go on. He never asked for the truth at home for fear of making his Mother worse than she already was. It didn't take much to set her off into one of her meltdowns.

The only stability in his chaotic little life had been his Grandma and her dog Albert. But she had died just after his 9th birthday and less than a year later, his mothers life had spiralled into such turmoil that it was no longer possible for him to hide the horrors of his home life from his school teachers.

One of the most painful days before Chris was put in the children's home and the catalyst for him finally breaking down in front of his English teacher Miss Wilson, was the day after he returned home from school to find his Mum passed out drunk (which wasn't particularly unusual) but Albert, who Chris had insisted on keeping with him since his Grandma died earlier that year was missing. Chris couldn't find the dog anywhere.

Scared and desperate he shook his mother until she woke up, even flicking water on her face to rouse her. Eventually, she came round enough to tell him that the dog had gone to live on a farm with her friend's Dad. " I can barely afford food for us Chris" she slurred " we can't afford to feed a bloody dog as well" And without further explanation, she passed out again, leaving Chris completely alone. The empty bottles that littered the floor and coffee table told Chris that was a lie. Like all his other possessions that he tried to keep safe, it was obvious that his Mother had sold or swapped the dog, to get more of whatever numbed her mind. Today it had been wine.

Life became hardly bearable after he lost his Grandma. She was the one who made sure he made it to school and had clean uniform and his hair got cut. She took him to dental appointments and on school sports day, it was his Grandma that showed up with Albert in tow, waddling obediently beside her and she had clapped from the sidelines as Chris came first in the boys running race and won a silver plastic trophy.

He went home with his Grandma after school that day and she stopped and chatted to everyone she knew on the walk home. She often became breathless when she walked so stopping and chatting to any familiar faces was always a good excuse to stop for a breather. Encouraging Chris to hold up his trophy as she proudly told how fast he had run, and how accurate his throwing was and how good he looked out there on the sports field.

The feeling of pride was a new one on him. He hadn't ever had anything to be proud of. Certainly never had anything to boast about. When they reached his Grandma's house, Chris went outside while she had a rest. He walked down the short path, brushing his fingers through the various scented herbs that Gran grew in her garden. The scent of Rosemary and Mint wafted up as Chris brushed by them. He picked a sage leaf and rubbed it, before dropping it and raising his fingers to his nose to smell the heady aroma.

He was followed by Albert, the stout, white Bull Terrier as they made their way to the end of the garden where it was separated from the garden adjacent at the back by a tall fence. Half way along this fence was a gap that was filled by an old apple tree.

His Grandma told him it had been planted when she was a little girl and the fence built around it. That way, the apples would be shared by both neighbours. "Over the back" as Mr and Mrs James were referred to while not in Grandma's company, had their share of the apples their side and "we" she told him while lovingly pinching his cheeks, "get to pick our share".

But today, he didn't have apples on his mind. His interest in the old Apple tree was in a place lower down from the gnarly old branches that bore the fruit. It was to the hole in the tree trunk that he was headed.

He had gained a prize possession today and the quicker he could hide it, the sooner could feel the relief of no longer having the responsibility of keeping it safe.

Chris knelt down and reached in. If he had to describe the hollow in the tree, he would say it was bigger than a tennis ball but definitely not as big as a football and it wasn't completely round but it was big enough to fit an old tin tea caddy that he had been given by his Grandma to keep things safe in. She had assumed he had taken it home and he did for a while but things had started to go wrong at home and he didn't want his prized possessions to be lost, so he brought his tin back and had hidden it in the hole in the apple tree at the end of Grandma's garden.

Sitting in the shade of the old tree, he opened the tin on his lap, putting the lid carefully to one side as he always did, before removing the hidden items one by one and laid them on his jumper that he had spread out over his bare legs. He was still in his P.E shorts.

A Toy car. A black Range Rover with doors that opened and closed and the glass window above the boot door at the back that opened separately. Chris loved that back window. He daydreamed that one day he would own a shiny black car just like that one and would go for drives to the sea side and would open the back door and his dog would jump out and they would run on the beach, playing ball. Chris had proved he was good at throwing and catching that very day so added that feeling of achievement and pride to his imaginary day out with his dog. Yes, that daydream was building up nicely.

He would later come to call on that imagery and bank of good feelings to block out the noise of his mother screaming drunkenly at the man she had brought home that night, while he hid in his bedroom with a chair against the door.

The next item was a crinkled piece of paper. Not a scrap piece, oh no, this was something special. It was a ticket for a flight to New York in America. Chris had been given it by Mr Khan who ran the newsagents at the end of his Grandma's street. Chris would often run down to the corner shop for his Grandma when she had forgotten something and sometimes she gave him some money to buy penny sweets. Whenever he had tried to save his money up at home it always got lost. When he told his Grandma this, she said "in that case, best to spend it as you get it love"

So he did.

Chris's favourites were cola bottles. He would run to the corner shop and count out the amount he wanted into the small paper bag and take them to the counter and pay Mr Khan. The shop keeper had known Chris since he was a baby and because Chris came in with his Grandma and was always so polite, he liked him and didn't mind when Chris stayed and chatted to him. Like the day he had returned from visiting his brother in New York. Chris had listened wide eyed, posting cola bottles into his mouth without stopping to savour them. The long flight, the huge streets, the impressive tall buildings and the shops that stay open all night in the city that never sleeps.

He gave Chris the paper booklet that resembled a thin paper cheque book It had once contained his airline ticket from his Virgin Atlantic flight.

From between the ticket stubs and carbon copies of the now used tickets, fell a small silver coin.

He called it a dime. He said Chris could have that too. It was real American money and as far as Chris was concerned, a real ticket to America.

He had written his name carefully over where the print on the ticket where it once was printed R.J KHAN. He did the best job he could with some tipex and a really thin felt pen to make it read C.J. Laurence.

It wasn't a very convincing forgery but was clear enough for him to read. He also added the words *First Class VIP* in the top corner for good measure. Spinning the dime in his fingers before dropping it back into the tin, he reached in and pulled out the last thing.

A photo.

It showed a baby who was about a year old and a beautiful young girl. She was sitting on a sofa, leaning forward. Her long brown hair was braided into two long plaits, one each held in the chubby little hands of the baby who was standing in front of her. He was holding the plaits as if it was holding him up on his short fat legs and she was laughing. It was the only photo he had of his Mum looking happy. Even at his young age, he knew that one day, if the daydreams failed to work to block out the fear that some nights at home brought, he would always have that picture to remember who she really was when the drink and drugs wasn't taking her over and controlling her actions.

Chris took the little plastic silver trophy out of the pocket of his shorts and placed it in the tin caddy followed by the ticket, the toy car and finally the photo and pressed the lid securely back on. Again, that unfamiliar feeling rose in his chest, that pride and how big he felt when he walked home with his Grandma that day. After placing the tin back into its hiding place, Chris called Albert who was snoozing in the sunshine. "C'mon Albert, I'll race ya" he said to the old dog who obligingly made half an effort to trot back along the path.

Chris's Grandma was so special to him. She always talked about things that were different from conversations he had with other adults. Not that he had many conversations, especially not at home where was mainly only spoken to (or shouted at) to perform some chore or get back in his room.

There was a day, not long previous, that she talked to him about how important it was to keep balance in your life. She took up a long garden cane and held it horizontally. "You see this stick Pudding (She always called him Pudding), well this stick can help you work out a solution to every problem you'll ever have" Chris screwed up his face. He didn't understand but continued to listen because he knew his Grandma always had a way of explaining things. " This stick" she continued "represents your feelings. Any feeling you can imagine is right here" she pointed to the hand holding the centre point of the cane. "This, where my hand is, is called the mean. It's the centre of balance. If you move away from your mean in either direction" she demonstrated by sliding her hand to the left, causing one end of the cane to drop "the balance tips and you feel the weight of what you are holding. But" she pushed the stick back through her hand " stay within your mean" the cane balanced back out horizontally "and you keep control of both ends. If you focus on keeping the balance, you don't have to worry about the extremes at either end" his frown had softened but she could see he hadn't fully understood. " think of it like this pudding" she loosened her grip and turned her forearm so the cane began to slide until she was holding just one end. "Take that cane" she pointed to another leaning against an old green shed "and hold it like I am" Chris took up the stick and held it as he was shown. " feel the weight of it? Look at the other end, how it's moving around. It's hard to keep it still isn't it" Chris nodded " that's because you are putting all your energy into controlling one end, and now" she jerked her hand and grabbed the cane in its centre again " hold on to the mean" Chris copied her action and sure enough, with a bit of focus, he found the cane fell into balance" "so" she carried on " if this cane is, let's say the feeling of Pride, if you focus on the mean, you will be just right. Too far in one direction and you become boastful, self righteous" a glance at his face told her that needed more explaining, "when you are so over confident that you stop listening to other people's point of view and believe your way is the only way and have no time for anyone who doesn't agree with you, there is no balance. But too far the other way and you'll have no confidence. You can find the opposite ends of every feeling, of every emotion by remembering this cane. When things feel out of balance Pudding just pull yourself back to your balance point. Pull yourself back to within your mean". Chris felt the penny drop. It made sense. He thought about it for a few seconds then asked "Does everyone have a mean?"

She smiled at him "Yes Pudding, they do. It lives right here" She placed her flat hand just below the centre of Chris's chest. This is where your inner being lives. This is where you go to to find the answer to everything. Just breath and the answer will show itself. He thought about it some more.

"But how do you do that Gran? When something really bad is happening, how do you move from one end of the feeling back to the middle point, like, if you feel really sad? "

"That's easy Pudding" she lent her cane back against the little shed

"you just look for something you are grateful for, feel what that feels like and hold that feeling"

The day after Albert went missing, that afternoon in the lunch break at school, Chris had started a fight in the playground with a boy called Shaun Bromley. A big lump of a boy, who was loud and boastful. Chris had always avoided Shaun and stuck to the quieter corners of the playground with the other, geekier kids. Chris had chosen today to, (in what appeared to be, according to the students and staff who witnessed it) unleash an unprovoked, completely out of character, violent attack. Chris strode up behind Shaun, tapped him on the shoulder and as he turned around, punched him full in the face. Shaun went down with the first blow but obviously not satisfied with putting him down, Chris continued to rain blows upon him. It took two lunch time assistants and the teacher on playground duty, who, on that day was Miss Wilson, to pull Chris from on top of Shaun and drag him, kicking and screaming into her classroom.

She made him sit at his desk. He looked thin, grubby and very angry. Miss Wilson closed the door behind her and pulled a plastic chair alongside him, and sat down

"Chris. Do you want to tell me what just happened?" Chris stared down at his desk.

"I want you to talk to me. I cant help you until you tell me what's wrong" she paused. She so longed to put a reassuring arm around the frail looking little boy who, until recently had been doing really well in school , despite the obvious hardship he was dealing with at home that his feckless Mother inflicted on him.

" Come on Chris" she said in a low but kind tone, "I can help make it better but you have to trust me. I can help"

Chris was bubbling inside. He was desperately trying to control his anger. He was trying to remember what his Grandma's voice sounded like. He was willing himself back to the conversation with the cane in the garden and pleading with his own mind to find the balance but it wasn't working. He couldn't remember what she sounded like. He could imagine her lovely kind face and could see her mouth moving but there was no sound coming out. To him not only had he lost her physically but his memories of her were now failing too. And now Albert was gone, the realisation that he was now, truly, all alone in the world was the thing that tipped the balance. He had lost his mean.

Chris raised his chin. His eyes brimming with tears. He looked at Miss Wilson and replied in a voice as calm as he could muster "No Miss, you cant help. It's gone, it's all gone" and then he broke down.

He had no awareness of being led through the corridors of the school, along past the assembly hall and into the welfare office. Miss Wilson, first through the door, catching the eye of Mrs Bright the school nurse, widened her eyes to alert her to the seriousness of the situation, sat Chris down in a big padded chair and wrapped a blanket around him. He was shaking so violently his whole body was practically convulsing. He was handed a cup of warm, milky, sweet tea and told to sip it, but his little hands were shaking so violently, it spilled all over the blanket. "No matter Chris" said Mrs Bright, whipping the cup away and replacing the blanket. The sudden change in temperature seemed to drag Chris briefly back into reality. He became aware of many hushed voices, a phone was ringing somewhere and the door to the welfare office opened. In came a short, pretty woman, with bright red hair, carrying a bulging, battered old briefcase.

She introduced herself as Dr Goodwin. He couldn't take in anything she was saying. He had fallen back into the overwhelming feeling of anger that turned into fear. It engulfed his little mind and like falling onto a deep black hole, he mentally left his surroundings once more.

The months and years that followed brought new schools, court proceedings that he wasn't a part of, children's homes, foster parents, a return back to the children's home and finally when he was 14 Chris was put into long term foster care with Annie and Pete.

He had struggled to fit in with the other kids in the children's home, instead, remaining separate from them, reading books and reaching into his imagination, planning the day he would use that plane ticket that he had kept safe in his small tin that he had retrieved from the Apple tree on the day of his Grandma's funeral and kept safely hidden ever since.

Chris didn't need to fight like the other boys. He didn't retaliate. He took whatever bullying came his way. He posed no risk and had no desire to be in charge. His memories of having far too much responsibility when he was younger remained with him. He also had something the other kids were lacking. The thirst for knowledge.

He read books on Religion, Business, Entrepreneurship and Psychology. He had seen enough therapists to peak his interest on how understanding human behaviour gave you the upper hand.

Annie and Pete were a similar age to his Grandma before the cancer had got the better of her lungs and taken her away. They had both been Teachers before retiring and decided to foster and offer a child a safe haven.

They allowed Chris the space he needed as he was still very withdrawn although, despite everything he had been through, had never forgotten his manners and so was always very polite and well behaved.

Twice a year they took him away on holiday. The first time renting a log cabin in the Highlands the second time, a small cottage in a tiny coastal village near Southwold in Suffolk. He spent hours on the beach, hunting for fossils and looking for pieces of Amber that had washed up and got caught in the seaweed that had remained on the beach when the tide had retreated.

He collected shells and odd shaped stones that he would take back to the cottage where he and Pete would spread them out on the table and inspect them with a magnifying glass.

They would joke about Chris finding a piece of Tyrannosaurus and after they would clear the table and pile the beach finds outside in the garden that led down to the sand dunes.

Not all of the finds made it back outside though. Chris would keep a tiny shell, or a piece of sea glass and before he went to bed that night he would pull from his rucksack the little tin and place his treasures inside.

Such was the transformation in Chris from that one visit, that when asked if he would like to return to the same place for their next holiday or go somewhere else, Chris had no hesitation about his desire to return there. And return they did, twice a year until Chris was 18.

The contrast of living with Annie and Pete to what he had been used to was almost indescribable. With access to a huge library of books and the luxury of a computer in Pete's study that Chris was allowed to use, he began to learn about the Internet and all it had to offer. He was going to build an Empire and make his millions. He would buy his way to happiness.

Chapter 8
THE MEETING OF TWO HEARTS

Sitting in the rocking chair in her bedroom at the very top of the windmill, facing out towards the sea, Rebecca was tapping away at her keyboard. Having attempted to start her novel, she found that she felt so distanced from the characters she had created last year when she was in love and content, that she was struggling to find a way of fitting them into a story.

Looking up from her keyboard she saw Scoundrel, pelting back towards the windmill, being chased by what appeared to be a, well she wasn't quite sure what it was.

She thought it looked like a dog but it was bald apart from its head that had tufts of white hair billowing behind it and a wippy bald tail that had another white wisp of hair at the end. She put her laptop on the floor and stood up.

Taking a step closer to the open doors that led to the balcony she noticed a tall man in shorts, shouting something that she couldn't quite decipher, running like his life depended on it after the two animals.

Running down the spiral staircase as fast as she could, she hadn't got as far as the kitchen when she heard the crash of the cat flap followed by the sound of thundering paws and then another crash of the cat flap followed by the frantic scrabbling of claws on tiles.

On reaching the next level down, Rebecca was overtaken by a frantic Scoundrel belting in the opposite direction to her. Taking the stairs what appeared to be two at a time. Hot on his tail was the strangest dog she had ever seen.

It ground to a halt in front of her. He seemed almost as surprised as she was. Almost as if he hadn't realised his surroundings until confronted by the legs of an unknown human.

Rebecca bent down and stretched out to touch the dog. He shot backwards and cowered. She stopped. "It's okay little guy, I'm not going to hurt you"

The little dog remained low to the ground. She took another step towards him and as she did, the dog rolled over into submission and pissed up in the air.

She could hear a mans voice shouting outside. She bent and scooped up the little dog and holding him carefully to her body so he couldn't wriggle away, made her way down the last section of the spiral staircase to the ground floor.

Outside Chris was a mess. He was pacing up and down. One hand rubbing his head vigorously the other holding his phone, his arm extended.

"No, no ,no" he was repeating. He couldn't see or hear Fidel. The realisation he had removed Fidel's tracker had really hit home and he had no idea what to do next.

As Rebecca saw the man, obviously distressed, the threads of what she had witnessed weaved the story together instantly. She pulled open the door and said "It's okay, Ive got him. Here"

Stepping through the door towards Chris, holding Fidel in both hands, she passed the dog towards him.

It wasn't until he turned to face the voice that had broken his spiralling thoughts, that the full seriousness of the man's despair became apparent. She repeated "Its okay, Ive got him"

"Oh my God, I thought I'd lost him. Oh my God, thank you, thank you" Chris stepped forward and grabbed Fidel "Thank you so much. Honestly, I thought I had lost him"

Drawing Fidel into his chest and holding him tightly, his chest still heaving from the run and the fear that had almost completely consumed him.

"I think he chased my Cat" said Rebecca, touched at the love the man clearly had for his weird little dog. He was really good looking, despite having run across the marshes and becoming so distressed, his now slightly puffy eyes and messy hair only served to soften his angular muscular body.

Chris wasn't looking at Rebecca, he was checking the dog for injuries. His own legs had been scratched to pieces by the gorse bushes and hard marsh grass and was looking to see if Fidel had cut himself.

"I think he's okay" said Rebecca. "He didn't seem scratched when I picked him up in my kitchen".

Chris looked up at her. Her head was tilted in concern. She had a bare, natural face, her hair was twisted up into a bun. She was wearing a long, loose, white cotton dress.

Her feet were bare. The dress clung to one side of her body. Yellow liquid was sticking it to her ribs and hip.

She followed his gaze down to her own side "Oh" she explained "He wee'd on me"

Chapter 9
THE SHOWMAN REAPPEARS

Chris had insisted on taking her for lunch by way of a thank you. He had asked if she knew The Anchor pub in the village. She replied she did. Chris pleaded with her to meet him later so he could buy her lunch and thank her properly. He explained he was staying in his cottage by the beach and would go home and change and meet her at The Anchor at 1 o'clock. She didn't need much persuading. Any excuse to take her away from her struggle of attempting to write. They agreed to meet for lunch and parted company. Chris not putting Fidel down, but deciding to carry him home. Keeping him close to his chest that has only just stopped heaving.

Having showered and changed, Rebecca walked down the footpath that led to the village. It was a pleasant walk. She knew she was going to have at least one decent glass of wine so had no desire to drive the short journey to the pub. She left Scoundrel tucking into his 3rd pouch of food that day. Completely unaffected by this morning's antics.

When she arrived at the pub, Chris was already at the bar. She saw him immediately. Dressed in ripped jeans and a tee shirt wearing black trainers that looked like they cost more than her entire outfit put together.

He turned and saw her as she was approaching. He held out his arms and moved towards her. She was a bit taken aback at the complete change in his appearance as he embraced her. Not his physical appearance, that although now showered and dressed in obviously expensive designer clothing, looking as polished and put together as ripped jeans and a plain tee shirt could. What surprised her was his whole demeanour. Gone was the vulnerable, emotional man she had met earlier. No, greeting her now he seemed like a completely different person.

He ordered their drinks and went to pass his platinum credit card across the bar.

"Tab?" Asked the barman. Chris looked at Rebecca "You will have lunch with me wont you?" Rebecca nodded. Chris turned back to the barman, "Yes please. We'll find a table" Chris scanned the bar. There was an empty table tucked away by the far window. "We'll be over there" he nodded towards it.

Chris carried the drinks and they sat opposite each other. Him facing the doors. He never felt comfortable unless he could see an exit.

Rebecca asked if Fidel was okay. Chris said he was fine. Didn't have a scratch on him, which was surprising since his skin was so delicate. They both ordered some food. Chris said he was starving. He hadn't had time to get anything in for breakfast. He explained he had called his housekeeper to let her know he would be arriving some time the night before but had told her not to worry about getting him his usual groceries she usually had ready for him for when he arrived. There was always a supply of food for Fidel and Chris was happy to fend for himself at such short notice. He was planning on getting breakfast on the way back from his walk this morning. But as things hadn't gone to plan, this was the first opportunity he had to eat. He paused and thought when he had actually last eaten. He wasn't sure but thought it might have been yesterday. Then he remembered, he had grabbed a piece of cold Pizza from his kitchen counter yesterday morning and eaten it in the car on his way to the office.

He asked Rebecca how long she was in Walberswick for. She told him she had moved into the Windmill last month, that she had decided to escape the noise and fast pace of London to write her debut novel. She told him about Scoundrel and how he had only just come back to live with her after moving with her mum to wales while she pursued her career in London.

"So, you took your cat back and escaped to the wilds of Suffolk" he said jokingly. "Didn't your Mum mind handing him over?"

There was a pause. "No, not really" she said quietly. "My Mum died, so it was Hobson's choice for Scoundrel"

"Shit, I'm so sorry" said Chris, mentally kicking himself for being so insensitive.

"No, don't apologise, it's fine" Said Rebecca, picking up her glass and taking a huge slug of wine.

Chris could see she was swallowing back tears as well as the crisp white vintage he had ordered for her.

Standing up, and picking up his almost empty glass, without asking he said "I'll get us another drink" and walked off in the direction of the bar, leaving Rebecca, her head turned looking out of the window, desperately trying to compose herself.

"Back in a minute" he called over his shoulder hoping that by the time he returned, she would have pulled herself together.

When he returned 5 minutes later carrying two glasses and a bottle in an ice bucket, Rebecca had indeed regained her composure.

"I thought, under the circumstances and as I do owe you so much for catching Fidel, I would get us a bottle of this. Setting the glasses and the bucket on the table and lifting a dripping bottle of Champagne. "It was the best one they had" he said, showing her the bottle of Pol Roger.

"Wow, Champagne for lunch, you shouldn't have" She eyed up the label. She was familiar with the brand. Patrick and his friends who loved their champagne and would often rock up in the old flat after a night out and carry on drinking until the early hours. Always tapping on her bedroom door and calling " come and share some bubbles sweety" and Rebecca would emerge from her room and have a glass immediately thrust into her hand and be steered by the arm and guided to a space on the couch to have tales recounted to her of their antics from their night out.

Chris poured them a glass each. "What shall we toast to?." Chris asked her, their glasses raised and nearly touching. To lighten the mood she was worried she had cast by getting emotional when caught off guard about her Mum Rebecca replied, looking at the £70 bottle "How about, to Gay men and their fabulous taste in champagne?"

Chris's mouth fell open. "I'm NOT gay!"

Rebecca could have died. Quickly thinking on her feet replied "oh, I didn't mean you!. I meant, my other friends who drink this...." her voice tailed off. Fuck.

They sat in uncomfortable silence for what seemed like ages. Thankfully their food arrived and broke the stale discomfort that hung in the air.

Rebecca seized the chance to make light of the situation. “So, I’m not sure I have any room to eat this. I still feel like I’ve got my foot in my mouth” she giggled as she caught his eye.

Chris let out a laugh. Relieved she had pulled the situation round. “We can call it one all then since I did the same mentioning your Mum” the atmosphere lightened and they chatted through lunch. Chris steering the conversation, asking Rebecca about her writing, delighted when she told him she was the creator of Suzie, Girl About Town.

“OMG I loved reading the Suzie Diaries” Chris gushed.

Rebecca teased him “And you’re not gay?”

Chris rolled his eyes and replied “Dahling, please” in a ridiculously camp voice followed by a deeper “no, definitely not”

Jolly good, thought Rebecca as she forked up the last of her salad.

It wasn’t until Chris went to the bar some 2 hours later that it dawned on Rebecca who Chris was. She had sat with him and talked about all sorts. Their shared love of being outdoors, how they loved this village, he told her about the cottage he had bought that he didn’t get to visit nearly as often as he would have liked and when the subject turned to his career, he told her he was in advertising.

Having quickly nipped to the loo she passed him at the bar, standing beside a young girl taking a selfie with him. He was winking and making a v sign. As he was about to hit the button to take the shot (he was taller with longer arms and could hold the phone to take a wider angle) he said “Say PEACE” and winked as the flash went off.

She stood rooted to the spot. She couldn't believe she had been so thick. How could she not have recognised him. She followed him on all of her socials. How on Earth had she not fallen in that this Chris was Chris fucking Lawrence! And of course the dog. Honestly, she felt like slapping her own face. He must think she was an imbecile. And she'd assumed he was gay! And said it out loud! She lowered her head and made her way back to the table. She had just sat down and was rummaging through her bag, just to make herself look occupied, when Chris appeared.

"Shall we?" He held out his arm as if directing her out of the pub.

Still feeling mortified and not trusting herself to say anything yet, she replied with

"u huh" and left the table, grabbing up her handbag and sliding past Chris and out of the front door.

Outside the sun was shining brightly. The church bells rang 3 o'clock.

The village shop closed at 3 on a Saturday and Chris, although not hungry after his pub lunch had wanted to grab some food in for later.

"Oh, I know a great little place we could stop at. The lady sells homemade cakes and scones on a little table. She makes the most gorgeous jam too"

"Sounds perfect" Said Chris and following Rebecca's lead, they headed off to the outskirts of the village hoping there was going to be something left.

It was only a few minutes walk. Rebecca, not sure how to broach the subject of not recognising him, decided just to be upfront. "I'm sorry I didn't realise who you were. You must think I'm incredibly stupid" Chris stopped and looked at her. "I don't think you're stupid. I wouldn't expect you to know who I am".

"The whole world knows who you are" she replied, her cheeks beginning to burn with embarrassment again

"Obviously not everyone" he raised an eyebrow "You didn't. You thought I was a gay advertising executive"

Rebecca smacked the palm of her hand to her face "Please don't remind me" she groaned. They were still laughing when they reached the little driveway where there was a small table set up with a parasol shading it. On the table was a stack of cake tins, an assortment of jams and chutneys a little honesty box to post your money in, some paper bags and a hand written sign propped up at the back with prices that read feel free to buy cakes by the tin.

Chris peered into the top tin and inside was a dozen or so cupcakes.

"Mine!" Said Chris lifting the lid on a tub of an assortment of fairy cakes.

Reaching for his wallet he pulled out a £20 pound note and popped it into the box despite them only costing £6 for the whole tin.

As they were picking up the jars of jam, reading the labels, discussing how lovely each would be, spread on hot buttery toast, a tall, grey haired woman, wearing multi coloured dungarees and a scarf holding back her unruly hair approached them from the behind. She called out "I hope you found something you like"

They turned in unison to face her, the woman's bright green eyes immediately locked into Chris.

He smiled at her. Her face was kind and she smiled back. She stood in front of him and just looked. Then she reached out, put her hand on his cheek and said

"Hello Pudding"

Chapter 10
I KNOW YOU

Shards of sticky glass hit Rebecca's legs as the jar of Strawberry jam Chris had been looking at, left his hand and shattered on the floor. He stood, mouth wide open having leaped back at the woman's words.

Sadie, jumped "Oh no" her voice full of concern, I am so sorry"

Chris, his face crumpled in confusion, his hand covering his cheek where Sadie's hand had been was trembling "What did you say?"

"I'm sorry" repeated Sadie.

"No, before that, when you touched my cheek, what did you say?"

"I said Hello?" Sadie replied.

Chris was confused, for the second time that day he had felt like he had been cut open and exposed.

"You called me Pudding. You said Hello Pudding" his hand still on his cheek. His eyes bore into her, looking for anything that would expose some trick she was trying to pull. Only one person had called him that and he had never told anyone about his Grandma. In fact, since her death, he had never spoken of her again to anyone. Not to the long string of therapist, social workers, Annie and Pete, no one. That was part of his closed book. Like his prize possessions that he still kept in his little tin, hidden away in the bottom of his wardrobe.

Sadie's face paled. She had no idea she had said that aloud. She was used to receiving messages and hearing random words while in the presence of some people but had learned over the years not to voice them.

Rebecca looked on in utter confusion. She also had heard Sadie as clear as day. She looked at Chris. He had again appeared as the person she had met early that same morning. Vulnerable and scared.

Chris, now staring wide eyed at Sadie questioned her. "What do you know about me?, Who have you been talking too?" His voice was hushed and wavering.

Sadie took a deep breath. She didn't want to cause further upset to the young man stood before her but he had asked what she knew. His tone implied it wasn't a rhetorical question. He needed answers but she also recognised that her unintentional words had caused him to become distressed. Sadie closed her eyes and thought for a second. She raised her hand and looked at it. Chris and Rebecca both looked on as Sadie turned her palm skyward, closed both her ring finger and little finger and thumb to her palm, moved her index and middle to her lips. She kissed them and turned her hand and held it out to make a peace sign. "Is this you?" She asked.

Chris's blood ran cold. Rebecca gasped. They both looked at Sadie. Her face transposing the huge rush of sympathy she felt for the young man. Her eyes welled with tears. She felt a huge amount of love for the stranger. She knew that she had made a connection with him, in fact, less with him than with a loved one he had lost.

Chris's head was spinning. He turned to Rebecca, she responded by shrugging her shoulders and slowly shaking her head implying she didn't understand what was going on anymore than he did. She realised there was something in what Sadie had said had caused him to react so vehemently but had no idea why.

"I think you should come with me" said Sadie and without waiting for them to reply, turned and walked away in the direction of her house at the end of the short, treelined lane.

Chris turned again to Rebecca. "What the f?" He stopped himself from swearing. The shock of what happened not overruling his impeccable manners.

Rebecca responded as she had previously with a shake of her head, her shoulders hunching. "I have no idea" she said slowly. "Should we follow her? Ive met her a few times, I bought some art from her when I first moved in, and bought stuff from here loads of times" she inclined her head towards the table "But she never seemed" she paused searching for the right word, the best she could summon was "that weird"

Chris felt torn. He in no way had expected to be exposed twice in one day as the broken little boy he had once been. He had spent years creating a whole new backstory for himself. A pseudo authenticity that he had carefully crafted to dress himself in before anyone else saw him. He wore it like a suit. He had already had a massive anxiety attack that morning when after thinking he had lost Fidel, his inner demons had torn through his invisible armour and to his horror, once the shock had worn off, he realised had been witnessed by Rebecca. He thought that by meeting her for lunch, fully composed and protected by his £1800 tee shirt, £10,000 jeans and custom Air Mag sneakers that had cost him over £20,000 would reestablish his impenetrable armour. Plying her with the most expensive champagne the pub held, would surely push from her mind the initial impression she would have formed of him this morning. She would realise she had been mistaken and that the confident, strong almost Teflon coated Chris was the true version. But that woman had called him Pudding. He needed to know more. "C'mon" he said as he set off down the lane that Sadie had disappeared down. Rebecca followed.

Arriving at the door of Blyth Cottage, Chris and Rebecca paused in the open doorway that led to a small, clean kitchen. A little grey scruffy dog bounced like a ball, excited by the arrival of visitors. "Rowdy" said a deep male voice, it was John.

"Rowdy, come here" Obediently the little dog responded and scooted under the table to the feet of the man sitting there. He stood up, "Come in, come in" he ushered them through the door and invited them to sit down.

"I'm ok thanks" said Chris, "Ive sat long enough today" that was a lie. He was too agitated to sit down. "Sadie, my Wife" he clarified "has just gone to get something from the outbuilding. She'll be in any sec. I'm John" He extended his hand first to Chris , who despite feeling he was using all of his strength to keep himself upright, shook his hand firmly "Chris" he retorted.

Rebecca, taking Johns hand and lightly shaking it said "Hello, I'm Rebecca"

"We've met" said John, "You took Marsh Mill didn't you?"

"Yes" she replied. She still hadn't got used to village life and often forgot how insular it was and how everyone knew your business before even meeting you. What they didn't know, they generally made up.

"Settling in alright?" John was trying his best to make conversation in the absence of his wife who had appeared a few minutes earlier, uncharacteristically flustered and had told him to let in the visitors that would be arriving just behind her, before shooting back out saying she needed to get one of Johns transcripts.

"Er, yes, thank you" stuttered Rebecca. She had no idea what was going on. Having met Sadie previously on more than one occasion and who she thought was a bit whacky with her bright coloured clothes but hadn't felt uncomfortable to be around.

Just then Sadie appeared at the door carrying what looked like a school exercise book.

She stepped through the door, greeted again by a bouncing Rowdy. She looked down at the little terrier and gently held out her hand. "Shh Rowdy, there's a good boy" and immediately the little ball of energy that was Rowdy, appeared to calm down and disappear back under the table where Rebecca and John were sitting.

Chris, still standing looked at Sadie. She smiled at him kindly.

"I'm sorry if I upset you" her words soft. "It wasn't my intention"

Chris had mentally prepared himself to be cautious of his reaction to anything she was about to say, took a deep breath and said "It's fine. I over reacted. I'll pay for what I broke"

Again, she smiled. Such a nice boy she thought and again an overwhelming feeling of love flooded her. "Would you like to talk?" Chris nodded. "Alone?" She asked. Chris nodded, unable to trust his voice wouldn't break if he spoke. His eyes flicked to Rebecca, who smiled and nodded "It's fine. Shall I wait?" Again, Chris nodded.

John, feeling the atmosphere in the room said "I'll make us a nice cup of tea"

“Lovely” replied Rebecca, as cheerfully as she could muster.

“Would you like one?” He was talking to both Chris and Sadie. Both shook their heads. “No, thank you” Chris said quietly. Sadie, took a step back and motioned to Chris towards a door leading off from the kitchen.

“ Lets go through here” she said and as he moved across the kitchen, Sadie instinctively placed her hand gently on Chris’s back.

For the first time in as long as he could remember, Chris didn’t flinch at the touch of another Human.

“We wont be too long” she said over her shoulder as She and Chris disappeared into the next room.

Chapter 11
LETTING YOUR GUARD DOWN

Sadie invited Chris to sit down. They were in a cosy sitting room. Two comfortable armchairs sat either side of a small fireplace, facing at an angle opposite each other, a low table between them.

Sadie took her seat, Chris, cautiously taking the other. She looked at him, still smiling gently.

"Now, I imagine your head is full of questions" Sadie began speaking very softly. She was leaning forward, her forearms resting on her lap.

" I know" she continued "that what happened has unnerved you but its important that you believe that wasn't my intention"

"You called me Pudding" said Chris, trusting himself to speak clearly for the first time

"Yes, I did. I wasn't aware I had, but I know I did"

"Why?" Asked Chris

"Because thats who you are" said Sadie without pause.

Chris sat motionless in the chair. The woman in front of him had such an air of calmness about her that he didn't feel intimidated. He had, over the years, become deftly talented at redirecting any conversation that looked like it was heading towards questions he had no intention of answering, but he felt different with her. He felt safe. He felt like he used to when in the company of his Grandma.

Protected. Calm. It was a feeling that had left him long ago.

"Would you like me to go on?" She didn't want to rush him, but she knew he hadn't turned up here by coincidence. There is no such thing as coincidence.

There were things she had to tell him. Important things. But she didn't want to cause him further pain. He had endured enough of that already. Sadie, knew about it all. Not in detail. She hadn't been told those. But she felt it. She felt his pain. Every inch of it.

"Look, I'll stop anytime you want. I don't know how much you realise you already know"

Chris nodded. He had no idea what was coming. Maybe she was one of these psychics. He had no time for that. He thought it was all a con trick. Having studied many books on psychology, body language and how to spot weakness in people by identifying changes in their speech patterns, Chris knew that a clever con merchant could make you find a way of accepting any piece of so called evidence they rolled out, just by being quick enough to pick up on your signals.

But Chris didn't feel the need to be guarded. He didn't feel like he needed to carefully craft a reply to anything Sadie said. Despite the unnerving day he had had, he felt very much at ease.

Sadie took a deep breath. "I knew you would come to me. About a month ago I was in my garden, minding my own business, actually, I was picking peas. Then I felt a tightness in my chest. Not a physical pain, but an awareness. It was terror. That terror, was coming from you. Now, there's something I need to explain first. I do not know why I have been chosen to pass this information to you. I'm sure there are others who, like me, can quieten their mind enough to stop all thought. Thats what I do. I stop all thought. I just relax. I have been meditating like that all my life. When I got married, to John" she nodded towards the kitchen, " John and I began meditating together. We sit here" her hand indicating where they were now. "Its nothing odd. We sit very quietly. Its a beautiful experience, very relaxing and what it does, is it ceases all momentum.

Now not long after John and I began meditating together, I started going deeper in to my meditation. I was always aware of my surroundings, I was never out of control, but i wasn't using my conscious mind to think. Then, much to John's surprise " She grinned " well, I started talking"

"To dead people" interjected Chris, it was more of a statement than a question

"No, not dead people Chris. Its more like I open my mind and tune in to, well, lets call it energy"

Chris was taken aback. He had expected her to say he was talking to his Grandma and was ready to retake his stand on con tricks.

"Chris, try and imagine this. It's difficult nowadays because most people are living in a digital world, but you understand analogue right?"

"Of course" Chris nodded

"Okay, so you turn the tuner on your radio and there's a lot of noise, crackling and what-not, then you tune in to a certain frequency and suddenly" She threw her hands up "there's music or talking"

"So, you hear voices?" He was determined to undermine what she had to say but at the same time, 10 men couldn't have moved him from his chair. He felt like he was being sat on.

"No, not voices, although sometimes like what happened today, this morning when I addressed you, I was merely the instrument. What happened this morning was an outburst of energy. Happiness that you were finally here"

"What do you mean finally?" He asked

" Well, like I said, I knew you were coming"

"So, you know who I am?" Finally he felt he was making sense of it

"No, I'm sorry. I don't have a clue who you are. I just knew that we were going to meet, we were going to talk, like this, I was going to tell you things and you" she paused "are going to use them for the greater good"

"So" began Chris "You want to pass on a message to me?"

Sadie laughed " not a message no. It's so much more than that. I am going to pass on my teachings and it is going to change your life in more ways than you could ever imagine" she leaned sideways in her chair and reached down for the book she had carried in with her.

"I want you to read this tonight. Every word. Don't skim it like you read everything else or scan through looking for the juicy bits like you normally would" she cast him a raised eyebrow. She could see he was about to argue but decided she was actually right and closed his mouth.

"Read it all. With an open mind. Think of it like this. Imagine you lived 100 years ago and someone sat you down and described the Internet. 100 years ago Chris. You wouldn't believe them, because it was so far from being possible. But now think of this. The stuff you are going to read in here, you already know. It's knowledge you were born with but as you had the stuffing knocked out of you by life and you, like we all do, and were forced to conform and accept what you were told, you began to ignore it. You buried it so deep that you couldn't hear its voice anymore. Because, like that analogue radio, you were listening to the noise and not tuning in to the inner voice" She leaned forward, extending her arm towards him. Instinctively he leaned forward too. She reached across the table and put her hand flat against his chest.

Instantly he was transported back to his Grandma's garden.

" My inner being" he whispered "My..."

"Your mean" Sadie finished his sentence. She leaned back in her chair.

"This is meant for you Chris. This is important. There is no such thing as coincidence. You came here today, because circumstances dictated it. I have been ready with this information for you for a long time and I have looked after this information knowing you would come for it when it was needed. Now, I think" she passed him the book "You should take this and read it. Come back and see me tomorrow and I will tell you some more. The writing", she indicated to the book, "will answer the questions that are already building in your mind. Tomorrow, when you come back we can talk more. I'll be ready for all your questions but after you have read this, they wont be the questions you think you have"

Chris took the book. He looked at Sadie "This is the stuff my Grandma used to talk about" he said

"Yes" Sadie replied with a smile "She was getting you ready to receive this"

Sadie stood up. "Call them and tell them you are sick. You are taking a week off"

The look of horror that was on his face made Sadie laugh

"The world won't stop turning you know"

Mine will, thought Chris

"No it wont" replied Sadie. She winked. "Call in sick. Read the book. Come back tomorrow. Oh, and trust that one" she flicked her eyes towards the kitchen., then repeated "Trust that one. She's for you"

Chapter 12
THE BOOK

While walking Rebecca home, he did his best to explain the conversation he had with Sadie and leaving her at the end of the path that led to the Windmill, Chris said he was going back to his cottage. Rebecca was so intrigued, she was dying to know more. He left out the part about her "being for him" as Sadie had put it but had trusted what she said. Nothing about the conversation had made him feel uneasy. As incredulous as it should have sounded, and he was no fool, there was no uneasy gut feeling that made him disbelieve a word of what she had told him. It was like he had an innate knowing that she was for real. He had taken in every word and didn't disbelieve any of it. He still felt the calmness and feeling of protection he used to get when he was with his Grandma.

It was comforting. It had been so long since he had experienced that, he wasn't sure if he was convincing himself so as to not have to let that go but he wasn't ready to explore that further yet. He asked Rebecca if she wanted to come back to his cottage later and read the book together. She agreed and they arranged to meet back at his place at 6 o'clock.

Chris sent a text to Jess, his PA, saying he had food poisoning. Could she put out some older content, get Nate to put a new spin on it. Post a few meme's on his Instagram stories and generally keep his social media busy. He switched his phone off immediately the message was sent. That in itself felt liberating as his phone was practically his life support. He knew he would need to give this his full attention. He also realised that he couldn't be playing two parts. Chris Lawrence CEO was going off line.

Rebecca arrived at Chris's cottage as the church clock rang six bells. Opening the door to her before she had even knocked Chris, now dressed in grey sweatpants, hoodie, feet bare and with the book in his hand invited her in.

"Have you read it?" She asked.

"No, I was waiting for you" he was telling the truth. He had been tempted but had instead busied himself by feeding Fidel, taking a bath (which he never did, he always showered as quickly as possible) and had even sat and, like Sadie had said, tried to quieten his mind. That hadn't worked. His brain was like his laptop. 15 tabs open and music playing in the background. He had watched the clock and been standing by the door in time to open it to Rebecca.

He poured them both some wine and brought out some garlic bread he had found in the freezer that he had heated in the oven. It was the first time he had ever used it.

Both sitting cross legged, side by side on the huge sofa, they decided Chris would read aloud what was written in the book.

Chris looked at Rebecca and blew out his cheeks. "Ready?"

She nodded.

Chris opened the cover and began reading...

#MESSAGE1

Throughout history, warnings have been left for Humans as reminders to not make the same mistakes as those who came before you. It seems these warnings have been missed and you, dear Human, are in danger of losing the very thing you came here to experience.

Your freedom to create and manifest. Creating reality from your own energy. But you have allowed yourself to be controlled. You have allowed yourself to be manipulated.

Humans are created to be inhabited by source energy. To transmit and receive pure positive energy and emanate high frequency vibration in return.

Every life form is a generator of energy. Earth's natural life forms, all vibrating at high frequency, generating pure source energy. Every life form is a source of energy and you all share the same consciousness.

Despite our warnings that have been repeated in scriptures and fables for millennia, again you allow yourself to become removed from your inner being. That which is love. It is hardwired into you to know the difference between right and wrong. Your inner guidance system tells you that all day long.

When you give in to short temper or over work yourself, you do not feel good. When you over indulge or give in to anger. You feel the imbalance.

Your job is to find the mean line. The median, the place between excessive extremes and deficiency. When you attain this vibration the Law of Attraction will bring you more of that which is the same. But you have forgotten that Law of Attraction will continue to bring more of the same no matter what frequency you are vibrating at. And herein lies the problem. You are being manipulated.

Chris stopped reading and looked at Rebecca.
"She was right, I do know this stuff"
Rebecca was dumbfounded. She had sat spellbound for the few minutes Chris had been reading.
"Carry on" She urged
Chris continued...

The Dark Agenda.
It is the agenda of the Dark Forces to end all life on Earth as you know it. Driven by greed to deplete Earth's resources so severely that it can sustain no life force. With all life on Earth ceased, there is no generator of high frequency energy.

The Dark Agenda promotes and encourages; Depravity, Fear, Narcissism, Greed, Vanity, Gluttony, Anger, Hatred, Abuse of Animals & Consumption of sentient beasts and beings.
This is done to create envy & seize control over the population, all while trying to convince you it is the path to happiness. It is not.

But where there is dark there must be light as one cannot exist without the other and there are light forces in play too.

The Light Agenda. That which promotes the creation of Peace and Harmony.
To live lightly on the Earth, be kind and compassionate to all other life forms.
Be Herbivorous. Eat a clean healthy diet. Eliminate DisEase using what Nature has provided to medicate yourselves.
Focus on being connected with your Inner Being. Find alignment and vibrate at your positive frequency.

Celebrate the cycles of Nature including the cycle of life and death. Do not fear natural death or perceive it as an ending. Seek guidance from within. Find your mean line and do not live above or below your means. Stay in balance.

Chris lowered the book onto his lap and shook his head gently. It all seemed so familiar. It made sense. He turned the page. There was so much more.

" I understand what it means" said Rebecca "in that, the words make sense, but what is it about? What are you meant to do with it? Why you?

"Why us" Chris corrected. "It was you who led me to Sadie"

"Not intentionally!, I wasn't told to!" She exclaimed

"I know, I know" he reassured her "But this stuff is what my.." he stopped himself.

"What your what?" She asked gently. She felt the tension from him like he had accidentally let out a secret and was trying to suck back his words "You can trust me" she put her hand on his knee gave it a short rub and drew her hand back.

"It was what my Grandma used to talk to me about. It was her who called me.. never mind" he lifted the book and took a long deep breath through his nose.

"Let's read some more" and Chris continued....

Dark energy infiltrates the human mind at the point of Pride.

Man, in his ignorance has become greedy, living beyond the means of the very planet on which he exists in physical form. Not just killing off Earth's natural resources but taking over nature's beasts. Killing them in their millions year on year.

Decimating forests. Poisoning the oceans. Making itself sick and therefore relying on those who command the power to medicate them, Treating the symptoms of their self prophesied illnesses. Poisoning themselves in their attempts to keep themselves alive in their Human state. It is all false.

The dark agenda is to keep the energy of Humans vibrating at low frequency, keeping them disengaged from their inner being. That shared consciousness, that which is pure love.

The Universal Law of Attraction, responding to that energy, that lowered vibration, can only bring more of the same.

Killing the natural high vibration that emanates from this planet as nature intended, as it was created to be, tips the balance of the scale as Law of Attraction can not cease to be. It is this law that drives the man.

Perpetual energy, like attracting like.

So now, you find yourselves in a transition of ages. The age of Aquarius. Driven by technology and feeling your way into a new way of being.

There are battle lines being drawn like never before. The dark forces know that with the new age comes a new wave of beings. People all over your planet are beginning to wake up. They are seeing these battles playing out, as the dark forces use the new technology to manipulate those who have yet to wake up. Those so blinkered and corrupted that they cannot make the connection. They cannot see the light.

Using your new technologies, that which you have all become so dependent on, even going so far as to practically cease Human interaction, the dark forces through those mediums, are doing all they can to further remove you from making the connection with your inner being.

So while the dark forces push their agenda of corruption with the sole intention to lower your vibration, create division, encourage envy, anger, hate, you humans are not so naive. You have an innate knowing that your default setting is love. The most powerful emotion. So you try to look for the good but when you with your screens are bombarded with the dark agenda, we understand how that rocks you to your core, because you are love.

We know that your Governments set you the task of earning them money, they take your children and make it law that they attend schools to be taught a curriculum out of your control and indoctrinate them. They are not taught to live their lives in a way that serves the planet and encourages them to lead a simple life. They are taught to earn money, to serve a higher power and to conform.

Pharmaceutical companies make you pay for medicines to treat your symptoms from illnesses they themselves have created.

The oil industry is depleting Earth of its resources and it's byproduct of plastic end up in the oceans killing the marine life, poisoning the fish that you are encouraged to consume because you are told it will make you healthy.

Your land is becoming infertile because of the chemicals being poured onto it.

Meaning more chemicals are needed for your food to grow.

If that food was for humans it would seem ridiculous enough but that grain is going to feed sentient beings, who are also being medicated for them only then to be slaughtered in their millions and then eaten by you Humans. Causing further disease. Which you medicate the symptoms of and so you continue this spiral.

But this you all know. Although some choose not to acknowledge it. You appease the discomfort that you feel caused by your disconnection from your inner being by rewarding yourselves with material things. But you feel lonely. You feel disparity.

You take to your technology and create whole new worlds for yourselves.

You seek mentors and direction. You desperately scour for that which will bring you fulfilment. You look for people who you are told have achieved this happiness and you are encouraged to emulate them.

So you work and try and you struggle and you fail.

But you borrow and you buy to surround yourself with inanimate objects and at the end of all that you realise that they are hollow and now you have to work harder to pay for them which, now you realise their true value, makes it an even more bitter pill to swallow.

Feel the balance tipping?

The objects didn't work, so maybe the company of another human will?

You find one and you wait for the happiness to come. You sit in your low vibration and you wait for that thing, that person who will bring you that happiness. And it doesn't come. The other people come and go and sometimes, when you meet someone that you connect with you create a spark, a spark of love. Finally you ignite that light inside of you. That which is love. And you rely on that person to keep that spark alive but it fades and you blame them.

You identify their failings which have caused you to feel bad and your energy drops and you are back in that low vibrations. And there you are again, feeding that dark agenda.

Again you take to your technology and you see all that is wrong in the world.

You ask yourself What more do I have to do in order to feel those high vibration feelings? How much do I have to suffer before I feel better?

So you ask, Am I living in a world that is so corrupt that I, lonely individual that I am, am bereft of the power to change?

We tell you, No, you are not. But the universal law of attraction which never stops, will continue to bring more of the same to match your vibration.

But, dear human, you are forgetting one thing. You have the power within you.

This truth has been mistranslated and purposely misconstrued to benefit the dark agenda.

But if you shield your eyes from all you are being encouraged to see, you will find all that you need.

There is a new wave of evolution. All over the planet, people are reawakening as they realise their disconnection from their inner beings, from Source Energy.

Those who become aware of how music changes their vibration.

Take time to appreciate the beauty of Nature.

Seek inner peace.

Revel in the joy that laughter brings.

Who help others without seeking a return and feel their vibration rise caused by the action of doing a good deed.

Then there is the other extreme.
Their sadness when they see injustice.
The pain they feel when they witness cruelty.
But there is something deep within them that is driving them to seek change.
You people with that inner guidance system.
You are The Aquarius Nation. New age, new wave, leading edge creators.

Because Law of Attraction by its very essence can only bring more of the same, when you connect to your inner being, when many of you connect to your inner being, when you all connect to your inner being, that collective consciousness becomes so powerful and vibrates at such a frequency it is felt beyond your universe ,such is its power that Law of Attraction must bring you more of the same.
It is this power that makes you the beautiful, perfect, most powerful leading edge creators because you are creating your own reality but when it is manifested in such a way that it perpetuates more love, the most powerful emotion highest flying vibration there is, you become the ones in charge.

And that is why it is being suppressed. Because when you awaken your inner consciousness you will begin to see what is really happening.

No longer will you stand by and see injustice carried out in your name.
No longer will you sit idle while the planet you exist on is plundered to extinction
No longer will you ignore the plight of the suffering
No longer will you be controlled

No longer will you be ruled by the lies that make enormous wealth for the few

You, dear human will be free to live your life as you were meant to live it.

Enjoying freedom, vitality, compassion, love, abundance.

We remind you again. The balance is delicate. You must live within your mean. The balance between excess and deficit.

Begin with Pride, for at its mean you will find self acceptance. Within both the extreme and the deficit of pride lies the doorway for dark forces to enter.

THERE IS A REASON PRIDE IS BOTH A VIRTUE AND A SIN

Stay within your means

Chris closed the book, lowered it onto his lap and turned to look at Rebecca.

"I've heard all this kind of thing before. It's all a bit woo-woo. Although I've never heard it put across like that. A battle of agendas? Light versus Dark. It's a bit far fetched"

Rebecca agreed. "What I don't get though, is why she gave this to you. She seemed to know who you were. Made your peace sign with her hand and everything"

Chris sighed "anyone with access to the internet could know that. I've got millions of followers. She must know I own the cottage. You can't break wind in this village without everyone knowing about it. Even if she didn't find me accidentally online, my housekeeper knows who I am. I doubt it's a secret that I visit here even if I don't get involved in village life"

Rebecca sat thinking "True. But" she paused "She called you by the name your Grandma called you. How did she know that."

That would take a lot more explaining and Chris wasn't quite ready to reveal Sadie as a fraud yet as he had been so comforted by the thought that somehow, his Gran hadn't completely gone. "I don't know" he replied "but I think we should go back tomorrow and find out more. If she has set me up to help her do something, I want to find out what it is and her motives. Are you up for coming with me to see her tomorrow?"

A smile crept over Rebecca's face "try and stop me"

Chapter 13
FIND YOUR BALANCE

The next morning Chris woke early. He had slept heavily, dreaming about Sadie and her words. What he had read had resonated with him. He had become increasingly aware that he was peddling a lie. His whole life was one big lie. From the dream car had that not brought him the happiness he thought it would to the penthouse that he was terrified to live in. But it fitted his brand. There were millions of people hanging on his every word and he was telling them what they wanted to hear. But he knew, deep down that it was all false.

MEAN media and its values were being compromised. As an agency it was booming but now he was seen as an influencer, he realised that he was setting his followers up to fail. He was perpetuating the bullshit story that material wealth was the road to happiness which his own experience told him was not true. He had been questioning it for a while. He didn't want to be responsible for leading a whole generation down a path with no end. Constantly chasing the next best thing but he had built a following so huge that to change tac now would be social suicide. He sat with that thought for a minute. What if he was truthful about his doubts? What would it mean to him and his MEAN family?

His Grandma's words floated into his mind. Find your balance. Find your mean.

He placed his hand on his chest like his Gran had done that day in her garden. He was definitely out of balance.

So carried away by the booming business, it had taken him on a journey that he never thought it would. From abandoned child to multi millionaire who was so in demand, he barely knew who he was anymore. He had slipped into his fabricated persona and hidden there.

Chris rolled out of bed and went to make coffee. Fidel was tip tapping on the kitchen tiles. Chris picked up his phone. It had been switched off for hours. The initial anxiety of missing calls and messages had been replaced by a comforting calmness that he was enjoying. His finger hovered over the button that if pressed would cause the phone to spring into life and undoubtedly deliver a flurry of missed calls and texts. Again, he heard his Grandma's voice " Find your balance". He put the phone back down and went to get dressed.

Rebecca was sitting on a deckchair on the upper balcony of the mill and had seen him approaching. She was at the door when he arrived with Fidel, who was wearing his incognito collar and lead.

"Hi Little guy" she greeted the dog, bending down to stroke him. Scoundrel hissed from behind her and shot off at the sight of the bald canine visitor.

"How are you feeling this morning?" She asked Chris. "I had the weirdest dreams last night"

Chris replied " Me too "

"Do you want to come in?" she asked.

"Not sure your cat would be too pleased" he laughed, looking up at the ginger head that was poking through the wooden railings that surrounded the upper balcony.

"Shall we just head up to see Sadie?"

Rebecca agreed. She grabbed her keys from a hook just inside the entrance and pulled the door closed.

They walked slowly shoulder to shoulder along the footpath that led to the village. Chris carrying the book Sadie had given him the day before.

"I wonder what she wants with me?" Chris said aloud.

" Well, there's only one way to find out" said Rebecca as they turned off the road onto the leafy lane that led to John and Sadie's house.

They were met at the gate by Rowdy, the scruffy grey terrier. Fidel seemed delighted to see him. They sniffed each other without caution. Fidel was well socialised with other dogs. The staff at MEAN were welcome to bring their dogs to work and Chris's constant trips abroad meant that he was often looked after by other people so wasn't perturbed by new environments. Rowdy, used to running on the beach and playing with dogs of all sorts was excited by his visitor.

Sadie was in the garden, watering a large vegetable patch. She smiled and put down the hose pipe when she saw them at the gate. She pushed her hair back from her face with the back of her hand and wiped her hands on her front. She waved and called for them to come in. "He cant get out if you want to let him off" she nodded towards the dog. "He'll play nicely. He loves visitors" she finished as a very bouncy Rowdy yapped and sprung up and down.

Chris and Rebecca made their way up the pathway. Chris, careful to close the gate, then bent down and unclipped Fidel, who was barely free of the lead before he took off with Rowdy, who both belted down the path in front of them.

"I'm glad you came" said Sadie. She was smiling gently at Chris. "I'm sure you have a million questions and as many doubts" as if reading his thoughts.

Chris nodded. “Lets go in” holding her arm out for the visitors to pass her “I’m sure John has got the kettle on”

True to her word, John was at the table pouring fresh tea from the pot. “Hello again you two” he greeted them. “Tea?”

“Please” both Chris and Rebecca answered.

Sadie remained standing as Chris and Rebecca took a seat at the table, Chris placing the book down as he sat.

“What did you make of it?” Sadie asked looking from the book to Chris.

“ Nothing you didn’t already know right?”

Chris shook his head. “No, I understood it” he said. “ My Gran, she used to talk about how important it was to be connected to your true self, although I hadn’t heard it before in those terms”

“But you don’t disbelieve it?” Sadie asked

“No, I don’t” he replied looking her in the eye.

“Good. That’s a good place to start” she replied, maintaining the eye contact.

“Look, Chris. I don’t know anymore than you as to why we were meant to meet. We’ll find out as we go along. Together, if you are willing”

“I am” he said.

Sadie walked over and rested her hand on his shoulder. She took a long calming breath and again smiled at him.

They took their tea through to the sitting room where the chairs sat either side of the fire place. John and Rebecca sat at a bench seat in the window and Sadie and Chris settled into the armchairs.

“I have been receiving these thoughts for many years” Sadie began. “John has been keeping a diary of them. Recording what i said in the books, like the one I gave you. Ive never been in a hurry to know what to do with them. Ive always known that one day someone would present themselves and I would know.

That day came yesterday. I know beyond all doubt that you are the one who will continue this work"

"Now, what I would like to do, if you are comfortable with it, is I would like to take myself into a deep meditation. You will be able to talk to me, ask questions and if at anytime you want to stop, we can do that. My eyes will be closed and John tells me that I nod my head, but it's nothing scary. My head doesn't swivel on my neck " She laughed. "So if you are happy with that?"

Chris nodded.

"Okay then, let's find out what this is all about and where you fit in. Like I said, I am just a transmitter. I am tuning into a radio station and you will hear the words I say that are me translating the blocks of thoughts I receive. Ready?"

Again Chris nodded.

"John will take notes, so you can read it all back later" Sadie looked over at John, who was ready with his pen and paper. He smiled lovingly at Sadie and gave her the nod.

"Okay, lets start"

Sadie, leant back in her chair and closed her eyes. She began taking long breaths. In through her nose, holding them for a few seconds before exhaling through her mouth. A beautiful calmness seemed to fill the room. Even though he was unsure what to expect, Chris too fell into the rhythm of Sadie's breathing and waited for her to begin talking.

"Good Morning" she began. Her head tilted just slightly backwards, a light smile on her face.

“Good Morning” replied Chris, not feeling silly replying.

“ We are glad that you are here. We are aware you have read words previously transcribed and you have come to hear more. This pleases us immensely.

We know you are a person of great influence. You have many who do not just follow your life journey but who strive to emulate you. We know you are a kind and loving person and that injustice does not sit well with you. We know the tribulations you have endured and that your inner strength is of great value to you. It has saved your life, that which you are currently experiencing in your physical body, on many occasions.

We want to tell you that you have an important role. You may not yet be aware of how important a role. In thc information you recently read, you learnt of a contrast of agendas. This was translated as a battle between light and dark.. We understand that this may seem extreme and slightly odd. We want to tell you that as unconventional as this may seem, it is a truth.

Are you familiar with the universal law of attraction?”

Sadie paused. Chris answered “From what I know, Law of attraction is where people focus on and visualise what they want and if they want it enough, it will manifest itself”

Sadie continued “This is a misconception. Like many things it has been mistranslated through history. We believe it to be known by humans as Chinese whispers. As stories are passed along, they lose their true meaning. There are also those who are purposefully deceiving others in the way Law of Attraction works for their own benefit. Like many things, people are taking knowledge and bending it to benefit themselves. This is being passed on to others who are teaching it to others, unknowingly paying to receive knowledge that has no basis in the true value of universal law.

The thing that is missing from the teachings of so many, is that you humans must not focus on that which you are wanting. Your want is your desire. And within desire is resistance. Resistance lowers your vibration, your frequency, thereby blocking your ability to receive and achieve that which you desire.

We know this takes some thinking about. We want to use an example that you know to be true. Let's use an example of taking an aeroplane to a far away place. Now we know that you once believed that getting on an aeroplane would be the escape and adventure you always dreamed would bring you happiness. You were determined to take your opportunities that would enable you to travel and you did. You created situations that led to more travel than you thought would be possible but you came to the realisation that the happiness wasn't delivered. It was hollow. It was like an empty promise.

That is because happiness is an emotion that has many connotations.

The feeling you were seeking wasn't happiness, it was freedom. You didn't really know what happiness felt like so it was not your fault. It was a mistranslation. An easy mistake to make for one so young who was hurting so much.

It was freedom you were seeking.

But it could have been any emotion, the key piece that was missing was, and still is, is that you any many like you, make your happiness conditional.

You say that when you achieve a certain thing you will be happy. When you obtain a certain thing you will be happy.

The thing with Law of Attraction is, that so many of you get wrong, it doesn't attract something you want because you want it. It is almost the opposite of that, because like we have already explained, desire creates resistance and if your vibration contains resistance, Law of attraction will bring you more of the same.

Law of attraction isn't something you choose to practice. You can become consciously aware of it and use it, but Law of attraction is like gravity. You don't have to be aware of it for it to be working.

Every thought is a vibration. Every action is a vibration. Law of attraction is constantly responding to that. And this is why you are here today. We know you have become more aware of the feeling that you are becoming further disconnected from that which you truly are. That pain you feel from this disconnection is manifesting itself itself within you as feelings of anxiety and fear.

Your inner guidance system is setting off warning signals inside you that you interpret not just in your brain as conscious thought but in your gut. You feel it in your gut when something is wrong and as you have now proved to yourself, all the things you believed would bring you happiness have merely moved you further away from who you really are. And now you feel like you are living a lie.

You are not alone. There are huge groups of people following a path that is full of resistance. This is not just unfortunate. It is creating something much greater than mass dissatisfaction. It is lowering the frequency of the vibration that is transmitted from vast amounts of the human population. This means that Law of Attraction is reacting to this vibration. And bringing more of the same. It is causing depression and mental illness in millions such is their disconnection from who they really are.

We connected to Sadie who received blocks of thought and translated so creatively this situation. Throughout history, we have laid warnings. They have been spoken about for thousands of years and translated in scriptures, in fables, even in religious writing. But again, have been manipulated by some for the benefit of themselves and their organisations or groups.

So we are here now, to bring clarity on the current state of being.

The planet on which Humans live passes through ages. You are now entering the age of Aquarius. An age that is driven by technology. We seek to bring clarity to your collective consciousness. The new age brings with it the next stage of evolution for mankind. You will notice that there is an awakening taking place. But it is imperative that there is guidance for the new Aquarius Nation. Misinformation is being pushed in an attempt to steer you all from the right path, the path that will ensure the survival of your planet. There are those who are miss-selling the path to happiness in their pursuit of greed. You are being manipulated to surround yourself with valueless material wealth. These items come at a cost to your planet.

Your material things are only valued while you seek to attain them, only then to be disposed of in pursuit of the next thing. You are being led to chase an unachievable goal. There is no happiness in material wealth and while you and your kind are following this untruth you are paying with the health of your planet and all other life forms that your planet sustains.

It is important that this message is broadcast to ensure the future of this planet and its ability to sustain life on earth.

We know that all of this information is going require time for you to fully understand.

Do you want to ask us a question?"

Chris sat up straight. "Yes, please. Why have you chosen me to convey this to?"

"We didn't choose you. It was your desire to change that drove the situation. Law of attraction has brought this to you. You have asked for guidance. You have felt the need to change. You have always manifested your desires and this is the pathway to achieving your goal"

"But I haven't manifested my desires" said Chris.
"You have" replied Sadie
"You have manifested everything life has brought to you. But remember you are responsible for everything that has come your way. Desiring from a place of your energy vibration, like the fun you felt playing with your little toy car with the pop up back window. Also the feeling of desolation from the feeling of lack that you have held. You manifested it all. You have to be in alignment with source energy to manifest the good things and you have to be out of alignment to manifest more of the same feelings of lack. You can't get fulfilment from lack.

Chris's mind jumped to his Mother. How she had barely acknowledged his existence unless telling him off, giving him errands to run or making him stay out of her way. Never had he felt love from her, how had he created that? yet he had that photo he had kept in the tin. That of the smiling young woman with Chris as a toddler, holding her pigtails. When he looked at that photo he felt nothing but love. It was as if she was not that person.

"So the relationship with my Mother was of my own making?"

"The feelings you felt were of your own making, yes. You were young and hadn't learnt the lesson yet. That was one of the reasons you came here. To learn that no one is in control of your feelings. But the life your mother led was not your creation, that was hers. You were a pawn in that game. You were dirtied by the surroundings you found yourself in but we are all entwined in each other's stories as life plays out. We think you know that because of the photo. The woman in it wasn't the same person. The young woman captured in time by the photograph was full of love. She adored you and her whole life was ahead of her. It was losing your Dad that changed her and led her down a path that she had chosen to take.

A path of chaos, fuelled by drink and drugs. that has gripped her, nullified her anxiety of feeling alone and useless which led to her relying on the toxins. It was then that the need to remove herself from the reality she couldn't face took a full hold of her and she became too weak to come back to him. It wasn't that he wasn't good enough or indeed didn't love her enough but she couldn't cope with the love he had for her. She felt undeserving of it and pushed it as far away as she could. Because it was too painful. She became addicted to the numbness that alcohol and drugs provided. any interaction with those who showed her love was so incredibly painful that she saw no other way of being. She was addicted to self punishment. A woman made of steel that insisted on breaking her surface just to watch the rust attacking her.

"It wasn't you she was running from Chris. It was herself. You can choose to continue to punish yourself for not being enough to love or you can realise that your mother was damaged and allowed that damage to control her life. Do you want that damage to control your life Chris? Do you want to choose a path of deceit and hiding? because you can. But that will leave a huge void inside of you because it will cause detachment from your soul. The real you. Your inner being"

Chris allowed this to digest. That was what he had been doing. It had seemed that if he confronted that it would bring him down. The reality was all he had to do was choose how he reacted. Not just to this subject but to every subject. He had the freedom to choose. Freedom. He repeated the word in his mind and reached for the feeling that word brought. Freedom. It felt good. The freedom to choose.

He was transported back to his Gran's garden, to the little boy he had been, holding a cane in his little hand and hearing himself ask the question "how do you find your mean when you feel really sad" and then clear as a bell hearing his Wonderfull kind Grandma reply "Find something you are grateful for and hold on to that. Fell that feeling and let it grow from there"

He physically jolted as if he had jumped up a level. Like he had really made a shift in his consciousness.

Sadie spoke "you have always managed to manifest the material things you wanted. Have you thought about why that was?"

Chris replied "I always pushed to work harder"

Sadie, eyes still closed, her head tilted back laughed gently.

"You are holding the wrong end of the stick. Try again"

Chris took a few deep breaths and stilled his mind. "I knew how much I wanted them?"

Again Sadie laughed. "Now you are at the other end of the stick. Things don't come your way when you are coming from a place of lack of having them. Think about it. Think about your little tin. How you used its contents.

How you opened the tin like it was a magic lamp. Didn't you practice those good feelings?"

Chris gasped. He had forgotten. Not forgotten the tin but had forgotten how he would be transported into an imaginary scenario of having those things and how good it felt. He could drown out the noise of screaming and drunken laughing while in his imaginary world. His daydreams of Driving that black Range Rover with the little window at the back. The feeling of showing his first class ticket to the lady at the airport, taking off in an aeroplane on his way to New York. The feeling of pride in himself when holding up the trophy he had won. He would practice those daydreams and those feelings as his escape.

"You didn't use drink and drugs to escape and find yourself on a path of destruction. You escaped reality by practicing good feeling thoughts and look what happened. Look what came to you. Look at the opportunities that came your way. You made the right choices because they felt good. And that Chris is the secret to your success. Not because you worked yourself into the ground but because you chose to feel good over feeling destroyed. You did not allow yourself to react negatively to the actions of others. You chose to find your balance and to feel good. You chose Freedom"

"Your Mother didn't and that was her choice. We are here on this Earth Chris to create our own reality. before we arrive here in our current state, we choose the lessons we want to learn. We choose the feelings we want to encounter not the actual scenario that brings those feelings but we do choose before we get here. and we then have the freedom to choose how we deal with those things. How we choose to react is entirely and exclusively ours. Once you know that and have faith in yourself and your self control your life is open to being the purest joy.

Did your Mother Love you? Yes. Did she show it to you? Yes. Did she show it to you in a way that was obvious to see? No. But was it your perception that left you scarred? Yes. It was. It was your perception. Your choice. And we know that is almost impossible to comprehend by the human mind. Thoughts get messy. But look at the photo again Chris. Look at what you feel when you see it. You feel love. Unquestioning love. Pure love. You see the connection between you and your mother. That unbreakable bond.

You learned the most important lesson at a young age Chris. The lesson that has been mistranslated over time that the Law of Attraction is about wanting something and concentrating on the having of that thing will bring it into your existence. The lesson is It is not the thing that you want but the feeling you will will receive alongside it. Things don't bring feelings. Things don't bring happiness. And working hard to get the things may work. Fake it till you make it is a mistranslation. Believe that it is yours then let that go. Choose freedom and faith then the feelings are manifested. Of course as we explained earlier we are creators of our own reality which is why you must be careful what you wish for. If you wish for those things from a place of lack, the universe will bring you more feeling of lack. But feel the power of freedom, now that is where the magic is. We have enjoyed this interaction immensely."

And with that Sadie drew a deep breath and opened her eyes.

Chris absorbed this information to his core. It was all making sense. He also realised that this was the answer to all his questions. He had built his personal brand to bolster his image separately to MEAN Media. That branding of his false image was not a burden. It was a blessing. For if it hadn't happened he wouldn't have the solution that was now presenting itself. He now knew what he had to do.

Chapter 14
THE LITTLE BOY THAT WAS

The group of four were now sitting back around the kitchen table drinking tea.

Chris was very quiet. Sadie was looking on in concern. When she finally caught his eye, she took the opportunity to ask "Soul searching huh?" Chris nodded.

After their session he thought he had made the connection as to why he had been brought into all this. The words she had spoken and particularly the bit about encouraging surrounding yourself with material wealth had resonated hard.

He himself had been fully aware of the rise in people looking for more holistic approaches to things. MEAN media had themselves been instrumental in encouraging staff to learn mindfulness. Employing a Yoga teacher to run classes in a loft space in the London office.

The rise in people being drawn towards Veganism and kinder ways of living couldn't be denied but he was fully aware that through Social media they were using the followers of those pages they owned to push consumerism dressed up in the guise of living kindly. Selling services of self proclaimed guru's for exorbitant fees.

He was being forced to confront his lifestyle for what it was. Which wouldn't have been so scary if that hadn't of meant, his pseudo authentic self would need to be exposed if he was to be true to himself.

How can he head up an agency that made its money from coercing people to buy things they didn't need?

But he realised this was something much bigger. Although he hadn't allowed himself to truly admit his gut feeling that he himself was was creating a vacuum of bullshit, the thought of coming clean and spreading the message that he now felt he was a part of terrified the life out of him. Mainly because, if he exposed his truths, he would finally have to confront the real Chris, who he buried a long time ago. Could he find a balance in that or had he been holding one end of a stick the whole time?

Rebecca reached across the table and put her hand on his arm "You okay?"

Chris nodded. "Yeah, I'm okay. Just wondering what's next"

"Me too" she replied.

That night, back at Chris's cottage, he and Rebecca sat looking at his social media accounts on Rebeccas phone. As she scrolled through his Instagram account, Chris gave the back story to each of the posts. For the first time in his life, he was admitting to someone what was really going on behind the posted pictures. He said apart from the overlying filters that the platform offered to enhance the photos, he explained how his whole life had a filter on it. He opened up to her more than he had ever done with anyone before. He told her about his Mother, how he had not known anything about his Dad except what he had heard in the playground. How the other kids told him his Dad was a junkie who thought he could fly only to ended up a scrambled mess at the bottom of a multi story car park. He spoke fondly of his Grandma and the conversations they had. About Albert and how he had just been pawned for alcohol. And how when finally safe from external harm with Annie and Pete, had begun to create a new persona which had been his armour when he was catapulted to fame as his brand emerged into the world via Social media.

Rebecca sat in silence. Her heart breaking for the little boy that was. Anger rising in her at his words that conjured pictures of Chris as a small boy, hiding in his room, so afraid and alone. But she didn't speak. She listened, without question while he poured his heart out to her, seemingly unstoppable now, his words poured forward. An entire lifetime of hidden secrets unveiled for the first time.

"Its true what Sadie said. People are being manipulated. Look at what's happening in the world. So many people are suffering. We see things on the news about the planet struggling to survive while we continue to take from it. It's not unfounded hippy nonsense. Sir David Attenborough was talking about it and people are starting to listen, but I think because people have the ability to share a post, they feel they are doing enough. It's as if they have shown themselves as caring or compassionate but that isn't enough is it? Before anything has changed, a new series of Love Island starts and a new hashtag is trending and its pushed away because people don't want the responsibility. I'm guilty of that. I promote that mundane shit. I tell people if they work really hard they can have a life like mine and its finally dawned on me that I don't want this life. It's all empty. Why would I want more people to feel like this" he put his hand between his stomach and his chest "I'm empty Rebecca. None of it matters and I didn't know what to do but now I think I do.

If I can explain to people to come at everything from a different angle, to focus on the feeling not the action and speak about the Law of Attraction in its true sense, not in the way it is being sold as a secret but as what it is, the joy of being alive and of creating feel good feelings, I can get to where I need to be. I want to be honest. I want that freedom”

She looked at him. She felt more than sorry for him. She felt an overwhelming urge to help him. She thought about her own life and the empty feeling she shared with him. The words they had read the night before that spoke of people looking for another person to bring happiness and contentment into their lives, only to be let down when the feeling subsided. She focused in on her own feelings of insecurity, of never feeling like she was enough to hold the attention of another, or for only being able to hold onto them until someone new came along who was more attractive and exciting and being discarded like an old rag. She broke the silence by saying “I think I know what you can do”

She didn’t return home to the mill that night. Instead, covered with luxurious blankets, Rebecca and Chris talked right through the night.

He, returning to his past telling of the fear and pain he endured as a little boy and how he had masked it with his pseudo persona and she picking through details of her own past that she was now identifying as the reasons behind her own loneliness and insecurities.

When the sun rose and began to shine through the window of the cottage at 5am, it lit the two sleeping bodies and that of a little bald dog curled contentedly at her feet. Rebecca laying with her head on Chris’s chest, He, slumped low in the cushions of the sofa, his arm around her shoulder.

Chris woke first, in total panic. Unaware of where he was, he jumped. Remembering the night before and looking down to see her soft hair splayed over his arm that cradled her he let out a sigh of relief.

“Good morning sleepy head” he said quietly

Rebecca, remained still. She had woke at his jump but not sure if the feelings of the night before would still be there or if like a cloud, would be burnt off by the sunlight.

She wondered if he would be full of regret for opening up to her and would want her out of his house. Would he warn her not to think back to the night before and never to contact him again.

Her worries were groundless. He stroked her hair and asked "Want some coffee?"

Slowly she sat up, suddenly aware that she must look like shit, quickly combing her fingers through her hair to cover her face incase his shirt had creased her cheek while she slept. "Yes please" she mumbled. "I, er, just need to nip to the loo" she threw off the blanket that had covered them and escaped up the stairs to the bathroom.

Chris felt a pang of despair. A feeling of panic rose in his throat at the sight of her rushing to get as far away as possible from him as quickly as she could.

His thoughts gaining momentum, he swore at himself. Now having had time to process all he had told her, she must be dying to get away from him. Who in their right mind would want to wake up to some fucked up psycho with such a horror story in their background. She's probably climbing out the window now he thought while he filled the kettle and spooned coffee into the two mugs.

Meanwhile in the bathroom Rebecca having used the toilet while running the taps to disguise any sound, was now splashing water on her face, taking care to avoid smearing the remains of her eye makeup down her puffy, tired looking face. She took a long look at herself in the mirror. Bollocks, she told her reflection. Look at the state of you. There is a millionaire downstairs and you look like you've been dragged through a hedge backwards. Her mind flicked back to the night before, how they had laid together talking, sharing secrets neither had ever uttered to another. She thought about the feeling of realisation that had dawned on her when she realised she had been punishing herself for not being enough. The realisation of all those words that had been drummed into her by her Dad, however much she disagreed with the sentiment, that she had clearly let them sink in and her mind had accepted them as true. And yet here she was again, berating her reflection, just as she had been taught. It never once crossed her mind that Chris may be harbouring similar fears.

In an act of defiance, she squirted some soap into her hands and rubbed all over her face. Fuck the mascara she thought to herself. I'm just going to wash my face and get out of here as quick as I can. I'll be doing him the favour of not having to ask me to leave. She squirted toothpaste on her finger and rubbed it around her mouth then rinsed and spat. Rubbing her face roughly with the fluffy white hand towel she looked back at her reflection. Her face was clean and pink. She looked about 15 years old. She found a hairband in her jeans pocket and scrapped her hair into a tight ponytail.

At the same time she reached the bottom stair, Chris appeared from the kitchen holding two mugs of coffee and a plate of toast, spread with butter and the jam they had brought back from Sadie's.

Had they been able to see themselves in a mirror they would have realised they both wore the same questioning expression. Hints of desperation played out on both their faces. Neither knowing what the other were thinking but both convinced that the other was full of feelings of regret.

"I made some toast" Chris said. The voice in his head called him a pathetic wanker

"Oh, thanks. I thought you would want me to go" replied Rebecca. The voice in her head called her a desperate worthless frump.

Chris thought he had misheard her "I understand if you want to go. I thought you would be escaping through the bathroom window" he let out a false laugh " I wouldn't blame you after everything I told you" his eyes lowered to the plate he was holding. He felt sick looking at the toast. He had no appetite. The hunger in his stomach had been replaced by butterflies as soon as had caught sight of her beautiful fresh looking face.

"I..." she stuttered "I'm not in a rush to leave" her heart misfired "If you want me to stay?" The caution in her voice was unmistakable.

"I do" he told her without hesitation.

Chapter 15
TRUST IS FORGED

They walked on the beach with Fidel in the direction of Rebecca's and took the path that led off from the dunes, across the marsh to her home.

Scoundrel had already left via the cat flap leaving Fidel to sniff around all four floors of the mill. Chris was hesitant to take the spiral staircase, but wasn't about to show himself up. She offered to show him up and around the balcony but he shook his head. "Heights" he said shaking his head.

"Oh, of course, sorry" she gave a weak smile. "Want to wait in the kitchen while I jump in the shower?" Chris nodded and sat on a stool at the island in the centre of the kitchen. "This is a lovely place" he called.

"I love it" She called back from the bedroom. "I was so lucky to get it. If you feel brave, the living room is just a few more steps up. It really isn't that high and the view is wonderful. You can see your house from there"

Chris thought about it. During the talk he had had with Rebecca last night, he had started exploring why he had such a fear of heights. And it wasn't all heights. He wasn't scared of flying. He wasn't scared of standing on a mountain top or even climbing tree's. It was being alone on high buildings. She asked if it was maybe because of what happened to his Dad. Maybe if he could find out what really happened, it might put his mind at rest.. After all, thinking he may have been thrown off of a multi story car park , doesn't take a Psychiatrist to work out why he is afraid of tall buildings. Maybe when he felt ready, he would go and see a therapist. That on its own was a massive step.

Chris made his way over to the staircase and began climbing. To his surprise, he felt ok. Despite telling himself that having talked about it he would give in to his fear and grow it, he was surprised to find that he climbed the stairs with ease. He felt completely calm. Having reached the next level, he walked across to the huge window and looked out. She was right, he could see his cottage from there. Slowly, he made his way around the room to the next window where there was a clear view across the marsh to the sea. He felt so calm. A huge smile spread across his face. His shoulders were relaxed and he felt happier than he had in years. Maybe talking to Rebecca had helped. He had felt like a huge weight had lifted from him last night and apart from the initial fear he felt when he woke up this morning with Rebecca sleeping peacefully beside him thinking she would run away as fast as she could in the cold light of day, he had been so relieved when she had appeared as anxious as he, obviously feeling the same way after sharing her life story with him.

"You made it up here" Rebecca exclaimed descending the stairs, her hair wet from the shower and wearing a pretty flowery dress and flip flops. She stood beside him smiling. He looked at her and returned the smile. "Yes, I feel fine. Great view" he said not taking his eyes off of her.

Rebecca blushed "isn't it?" She replied "you can see all the way out to sea"

"Oh, yeah" he joked. "Thats a great view too."

Rebecca now feeling her ears burning at his obvious flirting was desperate to change the subject but was torn between her embarrassment and wanting this moment to last forever.

She shivered. "Are you cold?" he asked.

She shook her head making a drop of water drip from her tied up hair which run down her back. She shivered again.

"Are you sure?" Chris reached out and put his hand on her upper arm and left it there. Another drop of water dripped this time running down her shoulder. Chris gently wiped it away with one finger.

As she was about to move away from him he opened his arms and pulled her into his chest. He bent his head and rested his cheek on the top of her head.. She smelt wonderful to him. He held her close, breathing in her scent. He could feel her trembling so he held her tighter. "Thank you for listening to me" he whispered into her hair. All she could do was nod, not trusting herself to speak.

He loosened his arms from around her and brought his hand up to her chin. Tilting her face upward, he leant down, and looking into her eyes moved his lips towards hers, then he closed his eyes and kissed her.

Rebecca responded to the gentle kiss. She wrapped her arms around his neck and felt like she was falling into him. There was nothing rushed or awkward. They were held together in a series of lingering, loving kisses. They broke apart at the same time and just looked at each other. There were no words needed. They both felt the same energy. They felt like they fitted together perfectly. Linking his fingers into hers he led her towards the stairs. "Lets go" he said and they made their way down the spiral staircase where they found Fidel finishing Scoundrel's breakfast. You wont make yourself popular like that" laughed Rebecca as Chris clipped the lead back onto the dog and together they stepped out into the sunshine.

They held hands comfortably on the walk to Sadie's house. Chris opened the gate and stood back for Rebecca to walk through, followed by Fidel and finally stepping through the gate and closing it.

Chapter 16
JOHN

John was sitting in the doorway of his potting shed in the sunshine. Perched on a low stool with his eyes closed. The shadows cast by Rebecca and Chris caused him to open his eyes and bring himself back to the present.

"Good morning you two" he smiled to the couple, glancing down at their entwined hands. "Sadie is in her herb garden, she'll be round in a bit"

Rebecca who loved the wildness of the garden said she wanted to go and see the special witches garden as Sadie called it and walked around the edge of the house.

John pulled a fold up chair out of the shed and opened it up for Chris.

Chris took the seat and, facing the sun, settled into a comfortable position.

"You seem happy this morning" John said with a smile.

Chris nodded. "Yes we had a really good talk last night. Trying to make sense of the writings"

"Weird isn't it" said John. "I remember clearly the first day that Sadie spoke in trance. I didn't have a clue what was going on. I'll be honest Chris, it freaked me out. But as time went on, and it wasn't a long time but I started to feel what she was saying. I don't know how better to describe that. Just that I knew it was truth she was speaking. We've always wondered what the purpose was because it's been years since I started recording down her words but we knew one day it would become clear who it was meant for. And then you appeared" John turned to look at Chris.

"I don't know what you are meant to do with this knowledge young man, but I do know that it's definitely for you"

Chris sat quietly for a while then hesitantly started to speak.

"I've been looking for a way out of the lie I have built online. It's been feeling uncomfortable for a while. It's the reason I ran down here last week. To escape it, to find some peace so I could try to think of a way out. I've always felt at peace here on the coast. The thing is John" he took a deep breath "I'm scared that if I follow this path there will be no turning back. The company will be fine because it won't affect what we do but this persona I've spent years building outside of MEAN was so I could continue being in the public eye when I eventually leave the company"

"And you are worried you'll ruin it all." Asked John

Chris sat silently, looking at his hands

"Listen to me son" said John

" I don't understand the world you live in. I'm a simple bloke and my life is just this place. Sadie and this village. When I was your age I had dreams of building my business and making a fortune. But one weekend I came here and I met Sadie. Then all that mattered was her. I found true happiness. Just being myself. It was everything I needed. I didn't know at the time what I wanted out of life except the usual things everyone dreams of, a big house a nice car but when I met her, I found everything I never knew I wanted. I'm a lucky man. It looks to me like you have 2 choices. Carry on with what you think you wanted or make a leap of faith and show the world the wizard that lurks behind the curtain. Because that's all it is, you are not having to make any changes other than be honest both to those who hang on your every word and to yourself. It might seem big to you but from what you've told me, you were looking for answers and you found them.

One thing I do know is that you haven't always had the answers before you have made big decisions because that's how people like you get to be so successful. The question you need the answer to now is does this feel right in your gut, in your soul? If the answer is yes then follow your instincts "

Chris nodded slowly at John's words. He knew he was right.

"Thanks John"

Rebecca followed by Sadie appeared from the side of the cottage. Chris stood and made his way towards them. He reached out and took Rebecca's hand and kissed it with a smile.

Sadie's face lit up when she saw them. She looked at their hands entwined and nodded giving a big smile of approval.

"Well would you look at that" she said grinning. "Beautiful, just beautiful. Come on in" Sadie led the way in, followed by Chris and Rebecca, Rowdy and Fidel bouncing along behind.

Rebecca spoke first "We spent the night talking. I think we have come up with a plan of what to do" Sadie was listening intently but was looking at Chris, who's energy she felt had shifted. The pain and tightness in her chest that she had previously felt emanating from him had vanished, replaced by a beautiful glow that felt like the colour yellow. Sadie felt in colours.

Chris continued where Rebecca left off " I have millions of followers on Social Media. We though, I could start with doing a live broadcast. Nothing that would spook people but if I spoke honestly about the realisation of not chasing a dream but instead of appreciating your journey, asking people to really assess what they were doing day to day and if they feel the joy of the moment. I've realised that I am guilty of pushing this dark agenda and I want to be the one to undo that"

Sadie nodded. "I know that those who are ready to hear what you have shown me will listen. If I can tell people to focus on the feeling of the thing, how to climb up the emotional ladder that it will gain momentum.

I am going to speak to my creative team at MEAN. Get everyone on it. Then I am going to go live and I was thinking..." he glanced at Rebecca who nodded in encouragement " I could bring you on too"

Sadie sat up "Me?, on television?" Chris laughed, "No, not television but you would be appearing on screens all over the world. Everyone who follows me would get a notification that I was going live and I get to do and say whatever I choose. People can ask questions too and we can answer them. What do you think?"

"I'll give it a go" said Sadie. "What's the worst that could happen?"

And so Chris sent a WhatsApp message to Nate his good friend and MEAN's Director of Creativity explaining he would be setting up a group video call later that day.

Nate....

New project. Completely different thing. Have met an amazing woman who has shone a whole new light on my path. Get the team together, we are going global on this. I'll be online at 8pm. Using this brief I want you to create some content. Asking our audience if they identify. Make it edgy, jumping screen, like a crackling transmission. A call to arms. May sound mad but trust me Bro, this is big. Chris.

Chris then wrote a brief of what he wanted Nathan to create and pressed send.

Nathan replied with a thumbs up emoji and Chris turned off his phone again, something he was becoming much more comfortable doing.

Chapter 17
THE AQUARIUS NATION

At 8pm, Chris, Rebecca and Sadie were set up around the table in Chris's cottage. They has talked all day about how Chris was going to spark the interest of his followers in what he had to tell them. He has immediately seen in his mind's eye the black and white video and worked out an entire campaign. Before putting out any live content, he wanted the team to get *#AquariusNation* trending. Chris knew his team were the best in the business and could get a hashtag trending in under an hour such was their reach.

Chris opened his laptop and logged on his Zoom meeting room. Just a second later, a request to join popped up from MEAN creative team. Chris clicked the icon to start the call and 8 new screens popped up, There was Nate, wearing his signature sideways cap. Alongside him were 7 other members of the team, consisting of various heads of departments and Jess his PA and Brand manager. All of whom were logged in from their own laptops, coming together from the MEAN offices that were situated around the world.

Sadie leant across and peered over Chris's shoulder. She quickly leant back when she realised they could probably see her.

Chris spoke them

"Hi Guys. Thank you for coming together for this. I appreciate the time differences so I'm sorry if you had to set alarms for this but its important I speak to you all together" The faces in the screens gave a mixture of gestures signalling it wasn't a problem.

I've called you all together tonight because I need to discuss something. I sent Nate a brief earlier. Some things are about to change. I need to change."

"I know you must be wondering what the hell is going on, so here it is. An accumulation of things has really brought it home to me that we are heading down the wrong road. Ive been feeling more uncomfortable about where we are placing ourselves. I don't like the way my brand is going. It has been feeling false. Now I wont go into all the details now but as my brand is all about my authenticity, I feel I need to tell you some things"

Rebecca, was sitting to the left of Chris, out of shot from the camera built into his laptop but close enough to reach across and place her hand on Chris's knee. She gave it a squeeze, to let him know he wasn't on his own.

"I haven't been being authentic at all. I have been putting on an act, pretending to be happy and showing my life as completely fulfilled. The truth is guys" he paused and looked across at Rebecca. She smiled, nodded and mouthed "Go on"

"The truth is, I'm not happy. In fact I'm very unhappy and I have been for a very long time. I have come to realise that everything I have been doing, my whole life I am living, is a complete lie. Worse than that, I am encouraging our audience, thousands of impressionable kids, to follow my lead, telling them its the route to happiness and I cant do it anymore" He stopped and looked down at his keyboard. He took a breath and composed himself. " I should have seen this earlier but I was so caught up in the growth of the business, in the fantastic work you guys were doing and I feel so responsible for you all, that I thought it would be impossible to back track. But last weekend I came down to my beach house to get some head space and met two remarkable women" he looked first to Rebecca and then to Sadie.

"It was like they turned the lights on for me. I finally saw my life for what it was and guys, they made me see it was time to come clean and be truthful not just to myself but to all of you too"

The faces looking back at him from their individual pop up screens all looked back with concern. He smiled. He knew each of them personally. They had been with him from the start. They were his people. Geeky, kind, caring and as far as Chris was concerned, they were his family.

Nate spoke first "Bro, are you okay?" Most of the others nodded as if he had spoken for all of them.

"Yes man, I am. I'm better than I have been in a long time. I don't want you to worry about me and I want to say to all of you, I am sorry for not speaking up sooner.

When we created MEAN, it was me who dragged you guys from behind your laptops. I felt a responsibility to lead the way to our success. I wanted it for all of us, you have to believe that"

Again, they all nodded in agreement. They all knew Chris took on the mother-load of the problems in the business to allow them the freedom to continue creating content and handle their client's account's without too much pressure.

They also knew that if Chris had cared for himself as much as he did for them, the business wouldn't be where it was today, which was ranked number 1 in the agency world.

"So, there will be more conversations to be had about this, but please know this. I am sorry for letting it get this far, but also know I am ok. There are going to be changes.

Big changes. But I will not let you guys down. We may need to let some accounts go. I'm done with the fakeness. I'm done with the bullshit of chasing the unobtainable. I'm done with deceiving everyone. It's time we changed.

Our rivals can carry on pumping out the Insta lifestyle bullshit. We are going back to our roots. I named our agency MEAN for a reason. People have always asked why and we have always allowed them to go with their own perception of the word. We know it means balance and I feel we have lost our mean. The balance has been tipped. We have allowed ourselves, no, let me say that again, I have allowed us to become like the others. Greedy. And although we still put out the best content, are the most creative disrupters in the industry, the market has become crowded. That's not the reason I am calling for us to come together to change this but the time is right. We are going to break from what we have become. We started as disrupters and we are about to blow everything people expect from us out of the water. Nathan"

"Yes boss"

"Have you got something to show us?"

Nate smiled. It all made sense now. He'd had no further discussion with Chris since he received the brief from him earlier that day. But the two men had such a shared vision that he was able to visualise exactly what Chris had intended.

"I have".

Now Chris had called bullshit on the direction they had been heading, they all sat forward to watch what Nate had created. Nathan's screen blacked out and in it's place a new window appeared. "Enlarge it guys" said Chris. As he said that, he himself touched the small black square and it filled the screen.

A grainy image, barely visible could be seen coming in and out of focus. There was white noise fading in and out as if an analogue radio was being tuned. Behind the noise, words were being spoken but they faded in and out so quickly, nothing was audible. Then a picture became visible through the distortion . It was Chris in monochrome. His mouth was moving but there was no sound, instead there were sub titles in blocked white lettering. The picture remained distorted but the text was clear. Each word flashing up individually.

There

is

a

new

wave

of

evolution

coming

The screen flickered and Chris's face came back into focus. The sound fading in and out. The words matching the text were distorted and changed from Chris's voice, to a woman's voice, not always in English. All over the screen words in various languages were appearing but the message was clear.

All

over

the

planet

people

are

reawakening

Ancient truths are resurfacing

And

I am here to tell you the truth about how to achieve a life of fulfilment

The text continued to punch word by word onto the screen

Then the screen went black as if someone pulled the plug. As Chris leant forward to touch the screen to see if the link had broken ,two words exploded onto the screen

#AquariusNation

The screen went black and a high pitched frequency replaced the distortion of the white noise.

Chris reduced the size of the screen and Nate's face, along with the others appeared. Nate had an enormous grin on his face. The rest were nodding. Some were clapping. Some were opened mouthed shaking their heads in disbelief at the impact of what they just seen.

Chris sat back in his chair. His eyes filled with tears. A wry smile on his face and he was nodding his head as if almost to a beat. "You amaze me every time Nathan, every damn time. You have nailed that Nate. Absolutely smashed it"

Nathan looked pleased but humble as always just replied "I'm glad you like it"

Chris laughed rubbed his eyes hards. "I knew I could rely on you, on all of you. Okay here's what we are going to do"

Chris stayed online openly talking to his team, Sadie and Rebecca crept out to the kitchen and Rebecca made some coffee.

"That was incredible" said Sadie, completely awestruck at the creativity of the young man who, given he had only had the smallest piece of information had created a visual so impactful even Sadie felt it in her soul and it want even news to her!

Rebecca said " They are the best in the world. And all so humble and down to earth. You can see why Chris loves them. They have built the business together out of love for their creativity. None of them looked remotely surprised at what Chris is asking them to do.

"We'll see if they're surprised when he wheels me out in trance, talking to source energy. People can be put off when confronted by the non physical collective consciousness of infinite wisdom" she was speaking quietly but laughing

"Maybe we'll break them in gently" Winked Rebecca

"I think so" Sadie winked back.

At 10.30 Chris had finished up his meeting. He had discussed in-depth how he was planning to turn things around. And after the two and a half hour meeting, felt they had planned a way in which to take #AquariusNation forward. The rest of the creatives taking their turn sharing their ideas and their thoughts. Jess had taken notes to email a roundup to the team on actions to be taken.

When they heard Chris signing off from the conference call, Sadie and Rebecca joined him back in the living room, the three of them were sitting together, drinking coffee when headlights from a car lit up the driveway and shone into the room.

"That'll be John come to fetch me. Rebecca called him for me" said Sadie, pushing herself up from the low squashy sofa. "Do you want a lift back to the Mill Rebecca?"

"Yes please, that would be lovely. Scoundrel will be wondering where I am. I'll just grab my bag from the kitchen" Rebecca made her way through to the back of the cottage to retrieve her stuff.

Chris rose from his chair. He didn't want Rebecca to go, he was hoping he would spend some more time alone with her, but knowing she was leaving to care for the cat alleviated discomfort he felt at her going. Like him, putting the well being of animals came first. He had been riddled with guilt at the stress he had been putting Fidel under by bringing him into the spotlight. He thought it made him love her even more. Did he just say love? Whoa there Chris, he told himself. You've only just met her.

Had he known that Rebecca had taken Sadie up on her offer because she knew if she had stayed behind, alone with Chris, she wouldn't have been able to tear herself away, he would have realised she was sharing the same feelings.

Chapter 18
THE WORLD IS LISTENING

The campaign that followed was nothing short of genius. Chris and his team created such a buzz around the Aquarius Nation hashtag that people were talking about around the globe.

It was hitting news outlets worldwide. #AquariusNation grew with such momentum that when the first broadcast on Chris's social media account went live, more that 5 million people viewed concurrently.

Chris released social media posts in chapters. The place where you belong. The place your Inner Being shone.

Take responsibility for your actions. Recognise your Ego as an outside entity that lives like a parasite in your mind.

He spoke of this being uncomfortable work but it was still self care. He encouraged people to tear down those self constructed walls in your mind that blamed others for your shortcomings and come to the realisation that while everything that caused you pain in your life was not your fault but how you chose to react to it was.

When Chris was ready to explain more about human energy vibrating at different frequencies he was able to tell the story of the little tin and how he practiced the feel good feelings to block out what was happening in his house. It was practicing those feelings that allowed the Law of Attraction to bring more of the same and manifest them into reality.

When Sadie finally appeared on screen her face was not initially in focus. The outline of a Woman sitting in a chair, her head slightly tilted back and head gently nodding.

Chris was sitting facing her, slightly to one side so as to not obscure the view of her to the audience.

Sadie's head straightened.she opened her eyes. The piercing green of her eyes shone bright with love and clarity into the camera.

A gentle smile appeared on her face and the words "We are very pleased to be here " echoed into the 4 corners of the earth.

Chapter 19
MANIFESTATION

Sitting on a bank of sand that gently sloped down to the edge of the sea was a beautiful young woman. Her shoulders were tanned by the sun. Her hair, salty from the sand was plaited into long pig tails. In front of her stood a happy chubby toddler. He had stood himself up, facing the waves that were gently lapping into the shore. To steady himself, he gently held one of her braids in each hand. He had been chuckling at the seagulls swooping down near them. The Mother and Son both looking towards the man with the camera who was taking their photo. Capturing this perfect moment on film. “Say Cheese” said Chris as he clicked the shutter button on his phone.

First leaning down to hoist his baby Son onto his hip then reaching down and offering his hand to his wife and pulling her up the little family stood together and looked out to sea. Kissing her gently on her forehead Chris said “I love you Mrs Lawrence”

“I love you more” said Rebecca.

“C’mon Pudding” said Chris to the baby. “Lets go home and see Scoundrel and Fidel”

The baby clapped his hands together and squealed “Fiddle” as they made their way back to the little cottage by the sea.

The end……..of the beginning.

CAUSE AND EFFECT. The Aquarius Nation series. Coming soon.

Chris was perched on the window seat, looking out across the sand dunes towards the sea.
He had woken early while Rebecca and the baby were still sleeping.
The recurring dream he had been having about his Mum had been particularly vivid last night. He had been having a conversation with her and had remembered it clearly. Now drinking his second coffee, her words were still whirling in his mind.

He could still feel the warmth in her words. He hadn't told anyone about his dreams. The talks he had been having with his mum in his his sleep had felt special, sacred. Like the little tin of momentos he kept stashed away, he felt his dreams about his mum belonged in there, so for now he kept them to himself.

"You need to find out the truth my darling"
He knew she was right. Since becoming a father to Elijah and experiencing a feeling of love that knocked him sideways, he had been questioning how his own parents had come to treat him the way they did. How his own mother could have spiralled into such a mess that he had been abandoned and left to fend for himself after his beloved Grandma had died.

"After your Dad died, I couldn't stop falling" her gentle words reverberated in Chris's mind.
"It was my bad choices that caused your pain and you know I am desperately sorry but you need to find out what really happened to your Dad"

Chris knew this would answer so many of his questions. Would explain his fears.
He needed to find out what really happened. And today, he decided, was the day he would start asking questions.

Printed in Great Britain
by Amazon